Nurse Alissa vs. the Zombies VI: Rescue

Nurse Alissa vs. the Zombies VI: Rescue

Scott M. Baker

Also by Scott M. Baker

Novels
Nurse Alissa vs. the Zombies
Nurse Alissa vs. the Zombies: Escape
Nurse Alissa vs. the Zombies III: Firestorm
Nurse Alissa vs. the Zombies IV: Hunters
Nurse Alissa vs. the Zombies V: Desperate Mission
Shattered World I: Paris
Shattered World II: Russia
Shattered World III: China
Shattered World IV: Japan
Shattered World V: Hell
The Vampire Hunters
Vampyrnomicon
Dominion
Rotter World
Rotter Nation
Rotter Apocalypse
Yeitso

Novellas
Nazi Ghouls From Space
Twilight of the Living Dead
This Is Why We Can't Have Nice Things During the Zombie Apocalypse

Anthologies
Cruise of the Living Dead and other Stories
Incident on Ironstone Lane and Other Horror Stories
Crossroads in the Dark V: Beyond the Borders
Rejected for Content
Roots of a Beating Heart
The Zombie Road Fan Fiction Collection

A Schattenseite Book

Nurse Alissa vs. the Zombies VI: Rescue
by Scott M. Baker.
Copyright © 2021. All Rights Reserved.
Print Edition
ISBN-13: 978-1-7351312-7-6

Cover Art © Christian Bentulan

Chapter One

A SUDDEN JARRING shook Alissa out of her slumber. She awoke with a start, expecting deaders. Instead, she remembered her and Chris were aboard the Seahawk heading back to Warren Island. Chris slumped against the corner of the troop compartment, sound asleep. At least he rested.

The helicopter bucked a second time. Alissa grew concerned. She put on her communications headset and spoke into the microphone.

"Is everything all right?"

"We're fine," answered Robson. "It's turbulence from the blizzard."

Alissa glanced out the starboard window. It snowed so heavily she could not see the ground. "How high up are we?"

"Five hundred feet. We're experiencing white out conditions."

Concern became anxiety. "Are we in any danger?"

"We're flying high enough to avoid trees and power lines."

"How will we find the base?"

"Sparks left on a navigational beacon," answered Frank, the co-pilot. "I'm homing in on that. I haven't been able to reach him on the radio. More than likely the storm is interfering."

Alissa wished they had flown back to the *Iwo Jima*. "How long before we get there?"

"We should arrive in a few minutes."

Thank God, Alissa thought. She looked outside one more

time, unnerved by not being able to see anything but snow. Turning to Chris, she gently nudged him.

He opened his eyes and smiled. "I must have died and gone to heaven because I see an angel."

Alissa grinned. "We'll be back at base soon."

Chris tilted his head and peered through the windshield. "What's all that?"

"We're in the middle of a blizzard."

"Lovely. We fight off hordes of deaders to crash and burn a few hundred feet from our destination." Chris regretted his comment the moment he saw Alissa tense up. "Sorry. I'm joking."

"I'm not a fan of flying, remember?"

"You can add being an ass to the list of my many faults you keep tabs on."

Alissa squeezed his hand affectionately. "You're good at some things."

The playful banter ended when they heard Robson mumble over the radio, "Shit."

"What's wrong?"

"The lights aren't on at the hospital landing pad. I can't set down there."

"How are we going to land?"

"No problem. The lights are on in Islesboro. I'll put it down in the park. It's only a walk of a few hundred feet to the town hall. They can call an ambulance for you."

Robson turned the helicopter around and headed back to the center of the island. Lights came into view, partly blotted out by the nor'easter. Robson hovered over the park, choosing the safest spot to land. Slowly he descended, scanning the area beneath him for obstructions. A minute later, the helicopter set down with a jolt.

"Sorry," said Robson. "But as my flight instructor used to say, any landing you can walk away from is a good one. The town hall is across the road to our right."

Alissa squeezed Chris' hand. "Stay here. I'll get a ride."

"I'll go with you. It's not far."

"You always have to play it macho."

Chris winked and pointed his finger at her.

Alissa opened the starboard troop door. A blast of cold air washed through the troop compartment, bringing with it a swirl of snow. She turned to Chris. "Are you sure you want to do this?"

"I'd rather you carry me."

"Yeah, but no." Alissa removed her communications headset and jumped out onto the playground. Over a foot of snow covered the ground. She assisted Chris down from the helicopter and, wrapping his left arm over her shoulder, helped him limp toward the town hall.

STATIC CAME THROUGH Robson's communications headset with a weak voice trying to break through the background noise. He recognized it as Sparks. "Sky King. Do not.... Repeat... danger... at once."

"Did you get that?" Robson asked Frank.

The co-pilot shook his head.

Robson shut down the engines. As the rotors slowed to a stop, he spoke into his microphone. "Sparks, I didn't catch all that. Please repeat."

Sparks did. This time, the message came through clear. Robson ripped off his headset and raced to the troop compartment, leaning out the open door. Alissa and Chris were a hundred feet from the helicopter.

"Get back here now!"

"What?"

"Get back to the helicopter. The base has been overrun by deaders."

Alissa did not hear him clearly through the noise, but she didn't need to. The snarling coming from inside the blizzard and the shadows of figures racing toward them through the snow let her know they were about to be swarmed by the living dead.

Alissa and Chris turned around and limped back to the Seahawk.

ROBSON RUSHED BACK to the cockpit, slid into his seat, and turned on the engine. Frank monitored the systems. The engine ground back to life, the gears churning interminably slow until finally coming up to speed, the familiar thump-thump-thump drowning out the anguished cries of the deaders. As the rotors reached full rotation, the downdraft blew a wall of snow away from the helicopter, catching Alissa and Chris in the face. Chris tripped and fell face first onto the ground. The deaders were less than two hundred feet away and approaching fast. They would never make it back to the helicopter in time.

"What are we going to do?" asked Frank.

Robson had only one option available. He prayed Alissa and Chris would forgive him.

Pulling back on the controls, he lifted the Seahawk off the playground.

ALISSA'S HEART SANK when Chris slipped off her arm and collapsed. She bent over to lift him. When Chris tried to stand, the combination of snow and his wounded leg made him fall again. The charging deaders had closed to within one hundred feet. They would never make it to the Seahawk in time.

Alissa withdrew her Sig Sauer and fired through the snow at the nearest ones. In the white-out conditions, she had no idea if any of her shots found their target.

"Save yourself while you still have a chance," ordered Chris.

"I'm not leaving you behind."

The sound of the Seahawk lifting off ended any further discussion.

Alissa stared at the helicopter. "That fucking asshole is leaving us."

When fifteen feet off the ground, the helicopter paused and flew sideways. Straight toward them. Chris reached up, grabbed Alissa by the belt, and pulled her on top of him moments before the Seahawk passed overhead and hovered over the horde of deaders. The helicopter's downdraft blew most of the living dead several yards away. One deader in civilian attire had the clothes stripped from its body before being knocked over. Only a few of the more intrepid deaders still lumbered toward the helicopter.

Robson stopped the helicopter five yards away from them and descended to an altitude of four feet.

Chris dragged himself up. When Alissa tried to help, he pushed her aside. "I'm fine. Get the door."

Alissa ran over and slid open the port door. Five deaders attempted to climb through the starboard side that they had left open, frantically trying to get at them. She turned and helped Chris into the helicopter before boarding herself, yanking the door shut behind her. The five deaders had pulled themselves into the troop compartment and crawled to their feet.

"We've got company," she screamed to Robson.

"Hang on tight."

Chris wrapped his right arm around the supports for the rear seating. Alissa held on to the ring mount welded into the fuselage with both hands, her eyes widening in terror as the deaders stood and locked their gaze on her.

Robson lifted the Seahawk another fifty feet. Just as the five deaders attacked, he dipped the helicopter seventy-degrees to starboard. They slid across the angled deck. Four tumbled out and disappeared into the blizzard. The fifth clutched onto a strap at the last second, dangling halfway through the open door.

Chris reached across his waist with his left hand, unholstered the Sig Sauer, and pumped four rounds into the deader's face and upper body. It released its grip and dropped out of sight.

"All clear," he yelled out to Robson.

The pilot leveled out the Seahawk and headed north. Alissa rushed over and slid shut the starboard door. When it clicked into place, she leaned against the bulkhead and sighed.

Chris pushed himself off the floor and sat on the seat he had hung on to, strapping himself in. He put on his headset.

"Thanks for saving us."

"No problem, sir. We didn't come all this way to be eaten by our own people. Sit tight while I figure out where to go from here."

Alissa sat beside Chris and buckled in. The bandage on his leg was stained with fresh blood.

"How are you doing?"

"That run in with the deaders didn't help my leg any. It hurts like a son of a bitch."

"We'll get it fixed soon."

Chris shook his head. "We'll be lucky if we don't crash land somewhere in this storm."

THOUGH HE WOULD never admit it publicly, Robson felt the same way. Once he obtained an altitude of a thousand feet, he flew to the airfield on the northern part of Warren Island, prepared to set down there if need be.

"Sparks, this is Sky King. Are you there?"

"Jesus, it's good to hear your voice," Sparks responded. "I thought for a minute we'd lost you. Over,"

"Came close, but only the good die young."

"Where are you now?"

"Hovering over the airfield on Warren Island."

"Don't land there. The whole island is infested. Those of us who made it out are at Belfast Municipal Airport a few miles north of you. Do you think you can make it?"

"Sure," said Robson with more confidence than he felt.

"Home in on my signal. We'll be waiting."

Robson turned the helicopter toward Belfast.

Chapter Two

A FEW MINUTES later, Robson brought the Seahawk into a hover over the tarmac at Belfast Municipal Airport, maneuvering close to the terminal building. Alissa stretched to look out the windshield. Someone with a flashlight directed Robson where to land, the beam barely visible through the blizzard. The helicopter settled with a jolt. Robson shut down the engines.

Alissa headed over to the starboard door and paused. "Is it safe?"

Robson nodded.

Alissa slid aside the door and removed her headset. Two figures approached through the snow. One, a National Guardsman, carried an M4 Carbine. Alissa recognized the other as Doctor Carrington. He waved for them to join him.

"Come in. Let's get you inside where it's warm."

Alissa helped Chris to the ground and turned to Robson. "Are you coming?"

"In a minute. I have to secure the chopper first."

The terminal was a two-story building much smaller than her cabin back in New Hampshire. She assumed it was a former residence because a roaring fire burned in the fireplace on the far wall. Once inside, Carrington stamped his feet and shook his head to dislodge the snow, then brushed the rest from his shoulders. He wore sneakers and a light jacket. Judging by the way he shivered, the doctor must have been freezing. He gestured for them to join him by the fireplace.

Carrington rubbed his hands along his arms. "Where's the rest of your team?"

"We're the only ones who made it out."

"I'm sorry to hear that." Carrington noticed Chris limping. "How bad are you hurt?"

"Gunshot wound to the leg from a ricochet. Not much damage, but it hurts."

"We'll take care of that." Carrington glanced around the room and yelled, "Boyce?"

"Yeah?" The voice came from a young man in National Guard fatigues casting a makeshift splint around a civilian's broken arm.

"I have another patient when you're done."

"Be there in a minute." Boyce issued instructions to a teen-age girl assisting him, then left her to finish wrapping gauze around the arm and joined the others. A man of average height and build, attractive with piercing brown eyes and closed-cropped black hair, Alissa guessed him to be in his mid-twenties but with more confidence than possessed by most men his age.

"This is Lieutenant Carter Boyce," said Carrington. "Our medic."

Boyce nodded to Alissa. "Who's the patient?"

"I am." Chris pointed to the blood-stained bandages around his leg. "I took a ricochet in the leg."

"That shouldn't be too difficult. Follow me, sir."

Chris limped off after Boyce.

Alissa reached into her leather jacket and removed the two vials of blood wrapped in bandages. "We retrieved the samples you wanted."

Carrington took the package, his expression crestfallen. "Little good it'll do us now. We had to leave everything behind when we evacuated."

"What happened?"

"One of the nurses became infected by the virus, died while on her way to the ER, reanimated, and attacked the rest of the staff. By the time the military arrived, most of the hospital had been turned and overwhelmed them. After that, we couldn't stop the spread."

Images from that first day in the ER flooded Alissa's memory. She quickly pushed them out of her mind. "What about…?"

"Your friends? We don't know what happened to them. Colonel Williams sent a team in to rescue them but they weren't heard from again. They could still be alive. We know there are others trapped in the island, but how many and where is anyone's guess."

"Why did you leave them behind?"

"We had no choice," Carrington replied angrily, though his tone held a tinge of regret. "It's a miracle any of us got out. A bunch of us made it to the dock hoping to regroup and get the civilians to safety, but the ferry captain had become one of the living dead. The deaders had followed us. Most of the military, including Captain West, died fending them off so we could take a motorboat and escape. Thank God one of the civilians worked at the airport, otherwise we might still be wandering around out there in the snow."

"How many made it out?"

"Eleven, including myself. West made Sparks and Boyce go with us. The rest are all locals."

"Shit." Would this fucking nightmare ever end? "What about the survivors?"

"Sparks has been trying to reach the *Iwo Jima* but with no luck. Once he does, they'll send in a rescue team to extract anyone who made it."

"How long will that be?"

Carrington shrugged. "Even if Sparks could reach them, no one can fly in this weather. According to the latest weather report, this storm could last another twenty-four hours."

"Everyone on the island could be dead by then."

Carrington averted his gaze and turned to face the fire.

Frustration welled up inside of Alissa. She couldn't leave Nathan and the others to die, assuming they weren't dead. Not after all they'd been through. But her options were limited. No one here had any military training other than Boyce and Sparks, and they probably had not seen much combat. She doubted any of the civilians could handle themselves against deaders. Besides, even if she could pull a team together, she had no way to get back to the island.

Robson and Frank entered the terminal and, on seeing the fireplace, made a beeline toward it. Robson rubbed his hands and held them close to the flame. Frank knelt and leaned in close to get warm.

"That feels good," said Robson. "It's freezing out there."

Alissa had an idea. "How long would it take to get the helicopter ready?"

"It's good to go now, though where to do you expect to fly in this weather?"

"Back to Warren Island," said Alissa. "We're going to rescue the survivors."

Chapter Three

KIERA STOOD BY the window to Nathan's hospital room, staring out at the mounting snow. By now it was well over a foot in depth, with more expected. Normally she enjoyed snow, and not just because it meant a day off from school. Now it sealed their fate, trapping them in an icy tomb.

How could everything fall apart in a matter of hours?

Rebecca had sent her and Shithead to the cafeteria to get something to eat while she watched over Nathan. Kiera had originally planned to stay and eat there but, between everyone in the hall giving her dirty looks over bringing a pet to the lunchroom and her own guilt at leaving Rebecca alone to watch Nathan, she picked up two orders of food to go and brought them back to the room. Thank God she did. Within minutes of returning, one of the nurses on the floor reanimated and attacked her colleagues. The entire floor became overrun by deaders, followed by the entire hospital. By the time the military arrived to save the survivors and put down the dead, they were already outnumbered. She watched from the hospital room as the deaders took down the soldiers who then rose, joined the ranks of the living dead, and spread the outbreak across the town. Kiera realized that if she and Shithead had stayed at the cafeteria, they would both be dead.

Though her current situation was not that much better.

Six survivors were crammed into the room – herself, Rebecca, Nathan, and three National Guardsmen who had fought their way into the building only to be cut off from their unit.

Kiera had heard the battle raging in the hall and ushered them to safety at the last minute. Rebecca had taken Shithead into the bathroom to keep him quiet, a nearly impossible task with all the commotion going on, hoping the closed door would at least muffle the sound and prevent the swarm of deaders in the corridor from descending on their room. Sergeant Julie Costas joined her, trying to raise someone on the radio and let them know they were alive. So far, she had no luck. Corporal Michael Murphy and Private Bill Rogers stayed in the room with Kiera, their weapons ready to blast anything that came through the door. Unfortunately, Kiera and Rebecca had surrendered their weapons to the security guard in the ER, in hindsight a bad move.

At least for now, the deaders were distracted. A patient had been trapped in his room down the other end of the corridor, calling for help for the last hour and drawing every deader on the floor to his room. Still, no need to invite unwanted attention.

Murphy tapped Rogers on the shoulder and used the middle and forefinger of his right hand to point to his eyes and then the door. Rogers placed the carbine on the bed, made his way to the door, and carefully went into a prone position so he could peer through the gap between the floor and door. After a few seconds, Rogers got to his feet and held up four fingers.

"Shit," Murphy mumbled.

"Were you planning on making a run for it?" whispered Kiera.

"What choice do we have?"

"Even if we somehow made it past all of them and out of the hospital," said Kiera as she motioned to the window, "where would we go?"

"We hear you, kid," said Rogers as he retrieved his carbine from the bed. "But a desperate attempt is still better than rotting away in here."

The bathroom door opened and Costas stepped out, closing it behind her.

"Any word?" asked Murphy.

"None from command. We lost touch with them when the comm center went down. The good news is we're not the only survivors."

Rogers huffed. "How's that good news?"

Costas dressed him down in a firm yet quiet voice. "Anytime we get word some of our people are still alive, it's good news. Remember that, private."

"How many are there?" asked Murphy.

"At least seven. Two of us down at the dock as well as two of us and three civilians at the school. There's probably more, but those are the only one who have radios. None of them have heard from command."

"Does that mean we're on our own?" asked Kiera.

"Maybe not. It might mean they've not had a chance to reestablish communications yet. We've all agreed to give it another two hours. If nobody has heard from command by then, we'll coordinate our own efforts to break out."

"How?" asked Rogers.

"We'll fight our way to the docks, grab any boat that's available, and head for the mainland."

Kiera glanced over at the hospital bed. "What about Nathan?"

"I'm sorry, ma'am. There's no way we can take your friend without getting us all killed. We'll leave him here and secure the room as best we can. That's the most I can do."

Kiera nodded her understanding and looked out the window into the blizzard. She reached up to her shirt pocket, fondling the Spiderman figurine Little Stevie had given her before they left the cabin. It reminded her that her people had been through worse and they would find their way out so she could give back the good luck charm to her brother.

"DO YOU SEE anything out there?" asked Captain Jim Saunders, who sat behind the run-down wooden desk, nursing his injured leg.

Private First Class Charlie Ames looked through the window of the ferryman's shack. "Can't make out anything beyond a few yards with all the snow. Do you want me to go out and scout the area?"

"Hell, no. I'm sure they're out there hunting for us." Saunders lifted himself on the arms of the chair, stifling a groan as he shifted positions.

Ames stepped away from the window. "How's the wound?"

"Haven't checked on it in a while. Turning on the lights would bring the deaders down on us."

Ames leaned against the wall and slid to the floor. "It looks like we're stuck here until morning."

As much as their situation sucked, at least they were still alive.

Saunders and Ames had been part of the team Captain West had formed to cover the evacuation of the survivors from Islesboro to the ferry, an effort that ran straight into a pack of deaders. Of the forty-four people who set out from town, only eleven made it off the island, and God knows whether they reached a safe place. The rest of the military unit had been overrun covering the civilian's escape. Saunders had watched the captain be torn apart. He and Ames were falling back to shore when a stray round struck him in the left leg, rendering him barely able to limp. At least it had not hit an artery. Ames helped him to the ferryman's shed where they had been held up for three hours. Since then, the only ones they had talked to over the radio were two other groups of survivors on the island, one in the hospital and another at the school, both surrounded by the living dead. No one from the outside had contacted them, which meant everyone on the island was fucked.

"What do we do now?" asked Ames.

"We wait until morning and then try to find a boat to get off this island. Once we do, we'll get the others and head for safety."

"How are the two of us going to fight off an entire island of deaders?"

"Let's worry about that in the morning." Saunders gently pushed the chair into the corner and leaned his head against the wall.

"And what happens if we don't find a boat?"

Saunders shrugged. "We swim for it."

FROM THE SECOND floor of Islesboro Central School, which had been converted into living quarters, Lieutenant Richard Hoskins looked out onto the grounds. The roof of the school bus stood fifty feet away, its snowplow having been attached that morning. Close to a dozen deaders milled around it, the figures blurred by the storm. God only knows how many more were nearby, invisible in the blizzard.

Or lurking on the floors below.

"What do you see?" asked Sergeant Joanne MacIntyre.

"The bus is surrounded by deaders."

"Fuck." MacIntyre swore under her breath. "That'll make it that much harder to get out of here."

"Tell me about it." Hoskins stepped away from the window and gestured toward the three civilians – Bill Ramirez, a retired Air Force officer who had left the service after thirty years and settled on Warren Island; Patricia Simmons, the registrar for the town council; and eight-year-old Susie Hemmings, whose parents and brother had been killed in the first ten minutes of the outbreak and who survived only because Patricia got her to safety. Hoskins and MacIntyre had stayed behind to gather up as many stragglers as possible and join up with West's unit. By the time they were ready to move out, the captain's group had been overrun and deaders had broken into the building. Dozens of civilians and three National Guardsmen were turned within minutes. Hoskins retreated to the second floor, blocking the stairwells with furniture to keep the deaders from getting to them, and hid out in one of the classrooms.

As Patricia held Susie, who showed signs of being in shock, Ramirez joined Hoskins and MacIntyre. "What's the SITREP?" he asked in a low voice.

"As far as we know," the lieutenant replied, "there are only thirteen people alive on the island and no one knows we're here."

"What's the good news?"

"That is the good news."

"How are we going to get out?"

"It's going to be tough with her," Hoskins gestured toward Susie. "We decided that if we don't hear from anyone in the next two hours, we'll team up with our people in the hospital, fight our way to the dock, pick up the survivors there, and get off the island."

"What are our odds of success?" asked Ramirez.

"Do you play the lottery?"

"Yeah."

"You stand a better chance of winning a hundred million dollars."

Ramirez chuckled. "Why did I know you were going to say that?"

BEN CARSON STOOD by the partially open door to the motor pool garage, staring into the blizzard to make certain no deaders had followed Gary Collins from town. Five hours ago, Ben and Brad Smith had been called by their boss, Woody, to head to the motor pool and prepare the two dump trucks for plowing and sanding. Not long after, they heard a commotion coming from the center of town. Half an hour ago, Gary pounded on the door begging to be let in. While Woody leaned on the plow of one of the trucks and Brad sat on a fifty-five-gallon drum, Gary related the nightmare that had taken place in Islesboro. Ben listened while keeping watch, shocked to hear that the entire community had succumbed to deaders in less than an hour.

When Gary finished, Woody pushed himself off the blade and paced around the garage. After contemplating their next move, he exhaled heavily and ran his right hand across his crewcut.

"Is anyone alive in town?"

"I didn't see anyone make it out, but that doesn't mean people aren't hiding somewhere." Gary thought for a moment. "I saw one group of Guardsmen heading for the hospital and another made up of forty Guardsmen and townspeople heading for the dock, though I have no idea what happened to them."

Woody turned to Brad. "How long before we get the plows mounted and the trucks gassed up?"

"No more than two hours."

"Let's get to it."

Brad looked confused at Ben and Gary, then back to Woody. "You're not planning on cleaning the streets?"

"Screw that." Woody patted the plow blade. "We're going to head into town, save as many survivors as possible, and crush us some deaders in the process."

Chapter Four

A LISSA AND THE others stood around the terminal counter as Ken, one of the island's residents, drew a map from memory on a piece of printer paper, pointing out the primary locations such as the airfield, the ferry dock, the hospital, the town hall, and the school used as living quarters. When finished, he slid the map across the counter to Robson and Frank.

"Sorry, this is the best I can do. The scale is a little off, but the location of key places is exact. Can you use this?"

"It's helpful." Robson studied the map for a moment and slid it over to his co-pilot. "The problem is visibility is shit. I need to know exactly where I'm going so I can drop off the extraction team, fall back to the airfield, and wait to pick them up."

"You won't come back here to wait?" asked Boyce.

Robson shook his head. "The less time I spend in the air the better."

"We need to get to the hospital," said Alissa. "Where is it on this map?"

Ken pulled the paper back toward him, circled the hospital and drew in the surrounding roads, and passed it back to her. Alissa studied it for a moment and gave it to Robson.

"Do you think you can land us on the roof?"

"I'll do my best," Robson replied with little confidence.

"You won't be able to," said Boyce. "The hospital is more of a primary care facility. The air conditioning unit is on the roof as well as a radio tower to communicate with the mainland. The only place to put down is a small heliport out back or the parking lot out front."

"The parking lot is out," said Robson. "There could be cars there and I wouldn't see them until it's too late. What's the heliport like?"

"There's only five hundred feet between the hospital and the tree line."

"That's going to be tough in this storm."

"It still won't work," added Alissa. "If you set us on the ground, we'll be swarmed by deaders before we can get inside. Is there any building nearby with a flat roof?"

Ken took back the map and thought. He circled another building to the south. "Your safest bet is the central school. The roof is large and flat with no obstructions."

Frank shook his head. "If it's being used as living quarters, it's probably a slaughterhouse inside."

"I'll worry about that when I get there."

"How far is the school from the hospital?" asked Chris.

"It's about two miles," said Ken.

"Fuck." A sense of defeat washed over Alissa.

Chris squeezed her hand lovingly. "Covering that distance is going to be a bitch under the best of conditions. There's two feet of snow out there."

Robson nodded. "I have to agree with your friend. The chances of you making it that far in this blizzard and avoiding deaders is slim. Why don't you wait until this storm is over, then I can fly you right to the hospital and put you down safely."

"This storm could last another twenty-four hours. Kiera could be dead by then."

"Is that what this is about?"

"Yes. Kiera is in this mess because of me. How can I face her parents… how can I face Little Stevie… if I don't try my best to rescue her? And Rebecca and Shithead?"

"Shithead?" asked Frank.

Chris grinned. "I'll tell you later."

Sparks entered from the back room.

"Did you reach anyone?" asked Boyce.

"Not on the island, but that doesn't mean there are no survivors. This storm is playing havoc on all comms. I picked up the *Iwo Jima* because they have a stronger transmitter. Primary is frantic to know what's going on."

"What did you tell him?"

"I'm not able to reach them on the radio we have here. We're on our own."

Robson lowered his head. Frank mumbled "shit" under his breath.

Alissa turned to Robson. "It's your choice. I can't order you to go."

"If it means rescuing people, I'm in. As long as you realize that once I set you down, I probably won't be able to pick you up until you return to the school or make it to the airfield."

"Fair enough."

"When do we leave?" asked Chris.

"No way you're going with me," Alissa said forcefully. "You can barely walk."

"I'm not letting you go alone."

"She won't be alone." Boyce stepped forward. "I'm going with her in case anyone needs medical attention."

"I'm also going," added Ken. "I've lived here for over twenty years and will be your guide."

"Do you have any military training?" asked Boyce.

"Does Somalia and Desert Storm count?"

"You're in."

"It's settled then." Alissa looked over at Robson. "How long before we can take off?"

"All I need is to warm up the engines, clear snow off the windscreen, and de-ice the airframe."

"When's sunrise?"

Boyce glanced at his watch. "In just over half an hour."

Alissa folded the map and shoved it in her pocket. "We leave in fifteen minutes."

ALISSA STOOD WITH Carrington near the main entrance to the terminal. Robson and Frank were outside in the Seahawk warming the engines, the rhythmic thump-thump-thump of the rotors audible inside the building. Chris' weapons had been distributed between Boyce and Ken, the former getting his Sig Sauer M17 and the latter his M4 carbine. Boyce also carried a medical bag. Neither was appropriately dressed for the blizzard. Ken wore snow boots and a heavy winter coat over an old pair of jeans. Boyce had escaped in fatigues and a light utility jacket, having to borrow a winter coat from one of the civilians who would be staying behind. None of them heading back to Warren Island had gloves or hats. The weather would be as lethal an enemy as the deaders.

Boyce and Ken opened the terminal door and headed for the helicopter. Boyce paused to ask Alissa, "Are you coming?"

"I'll be there in a minute."

When they departed, she turned to Carrington. "Are the blood samples we retrieved from Boston safe?"

The doctor pointed to a cooler by the door. "They're packed in snow. That'll maintain their integrity."

"Good. In case we don't get the others back...." Alissa allowed her thought to trail off.

"I promise I'll keep them safe." Carrington reached behind the counter and withdrew a black baseball cap with the Air Force logo embroidered on it. "I found this in the back room. It's better than nothing."

"Thanks." Alissa placed the cap on her head. She searched for Chris but could not find him, assuming he sulked some-where. Screw it. She'd deal with him later. Alissa shook the doctor's hand. "I'll see you when I get back."

"Good luck."

Alissa departed the terminal, ducking low. The downdraft from the rotors churned the snow into a frenzy, blinding her. She saw the door to the Seahawk a second before she reached it. Climbing onto the flight deck, she reached behind her, slid shut the troop door, and secured it.

A familiar voice said, "Welcome aboard."

Chris sat in the seat by the port troop door.

"What are you doing here? You're in no condition to go with us."

"I'm Robson's new crew chief."

Alissa glared at him. "What do you know about being a crew chief?"

"The same as you about leading a combat mission."

Chris held out her headset and patted the seat beside him. Alissa took it, placed it on her head, but sat across from him. Chris gestured for her to pop the magazine out of her carbine and point the barrel at the floor. She complied, although she threw him a glare colder than the weather outside.

Robson's voice came through the headset. "Are we ready back there?"

"Roger that," answered Chris.

The intensity of the rotors increased and the Seahawk lifted off the tarmac. Snow swirled around the windows, restricting their view. After a few seconds, the helicopter reached enough of a height that it didn't generate a downdraft.

"Good morning, ladies and gentlemen. This is your pilot speaking. We have a short flight to our destination, so sit back and enjoy it while you can. We know you had no choice of airlines, but we thank you for flying Miracle Air. Remember our motto: If you get there, it's a miracle."

Chris smiled at the old joke. Alissa shook her head.

Robson turned the helicopter southeast and headed for Warren Island.

Chapter Five

ROBSON FLEW THE Seahawk over Penobscot Bay and continued south, making landfall on Warren Island near Turtle Head Cove. Both he and Frank wore Night Vision Goggles to help them see better through the blizzard. The horizon to the east grew lighter, indicating sunrise had occurred, although in this storm it helped only slightly. With visibility poor, he descended, praying he wouldn't hit treetops or power lines. He detected a smooth, white patch of snow running north-south through the trees. Assuming it to be the main road, he followed it. A few minutes later, they passed over the narrow strip of land separating the northern and southern parts of the island, the surf pounding on shore barely discernable.

Frank pointed ahead of him. "Isn't that where we landed two days ago?"

Despite being covered in two feet of snow, the contours of the airfield were still visible, though barely. "It is. We're close to the center of town. Keep your eyes out for the school."

BEN STOOD BY the door to the motor pool garage, staring into the blizzard, searching for any approaching deaders. Between the dark and the white out conditions, those things could sneak up on them undetected.

Something unusual caught his attention. At first, Ben assumed it to be the snarling of a horde of deaders. After a minute, it became more audible. It belonged to something mechanical, not living dead.

"Guys, come here." Ben leaned into the garage.

"Shut up," Woody yelled out from the front of the Mack where he assisted Brad in installing the plow. "You'll bring the whole fucking horde down on us."

"You got to hear this. It sounds like a helicopter."

"Are you nuts?" Woody put down the wrench and crossed the garage, followed by Brad and Gary. "No lunatic would fly in this weather."

Ben pointed to the sky. "Listen."

Woody stepped outside and looked up.

Brad leaned out to listen. "That's a helicopter."

Woody waved his hand for them to be quiet and listened. "It's a helicopter."

Ben shook his head. "No, shit."

Ducking back into the garage, Woody motioned to the others. "We have to get our asses in gear."

"What for?" asked Brad.

"To get these plows attached. No one knows we're here. If we want to get out alive, we need to track down that chopper."

KIERA SAT ON the floor in the far corner of the room, leaning against the walls, dozing. The deaders in the corridor suddenly became active, shuffling around loudly and moaning. She noticed shadows moving back and forth underneath the door. Kiera jumped to her feet, prepared to fend off an attack. Costas, Murphy, and Rogers had taken up position near the door, their Sig Sauers drawn. Rebecca stayed in the bathroom, one hand wrapped around Shithead's mouth and the other petting him, trying to keep him quiet.

Only the living dead were not coming after them.

"What's going on?" asked Murphy.

"Something got them riled up," whispered Costas.

Kiera heard it first. An engine. She moved over to the window and looked out. "You have to see this."

Costas joined her as a helicopter flew past, its outline blurred by the storm.

Rogers raised his eyebrows. "A rescue mission?"

"Looks like it." Costas stepped away from the window, took the radio from Rogers, and headed for the bathroom. "I'm going to check with the others."

THE RADIO CRACKLED and Costas's voice came through the speaker. "Hoskins, you there?"

Hoskins picked up the radio and pressed the talk button. "I'm here. What's up?"

"We just spotted a helicopter over town."

The lieutenant did not believe him. "In this weather?"

"I know it sounds crazy. Several of us saw it."

MacIntyre went over to the window and opened it. She listened for a few seconds but could only hear the wind. Then it came through, the distinct thumping of helicopter rotors.

"Damn it, there's a chopper out there. And it sounds like it's heading this way."

"Where did it come from?"

"Who cares? Hang on." Hoskins lowered the radio and snapped his fingers to attract MacIntyre's attention. "Get on the roof and flag them down."

"With what?"

"I have a flashlight." Ramirez pushed himself off his cot, stepped over to his locker, and removed an Imalent one hundred thousand lumen flashlight from the top shelf. "This ought to get their attention."

"Thanks." She ran out of the room and down the hall,

heading for the ladder that led to the roof.

"Costas, contact Saunders and let him know what's going on. I'm going to greet our guests and find out what this is all about."

COSTAS' VOICE CAME over the radio. "Captain Saunders, can you read me, sir?"

Ames pressed the talk button. "We read you."

"How's the captain?"

"Still in a lot of pain. And we're both freezing."

"You may not be cold much longer. There's a chopper over the island."

Saunders motioned for Ames to give him the radio. "What are you smoking? No way anyone could fly in this weather."

"Someone did. A bunch of us saw it and Lieutenant Hoskins' group heard it. They're trying to flag it down."

"Let's hope they do. Keep me posted."

Saunders handed the radio back to Ames then shifted position, moaning from pain.

"Do you think it's legit, sir?"

"What?"

"The rescue mission."

"I don't know what it is, and I don't care. As long as they can get us off this damned island."

ROBSON MANEUVERED THE Seahawk so it flew down the west coast of Warren Island.

"What are we looking for?" asked Frank.

"For the school. Ken, can you join us?"

Ken unbuckled himself and moved forward to the cockpit. "What's up?"

"I need you to help us locate the school."

Ken moved between the pilot and co-pilot. "Are you following the central road?"

"No. The coast road."

"Then it should be on the left."

"What's that?" asked Frank.

"Where?"

"Off to the left. It looks like someone's shining a flashlight."

"That's the school," said Ken.

Alissa came forward to see. "Looks like we found survivors."

"That's not necessarily a good thing."

"Why?"

"I can't take more than six passengers, especially in this weather. And I already have you four."

"Shit." Alissa had not thought of that.

Robson pointed to the main troop compartment. "Everyone, take your seats and strap in. This landing is going to be rough."

HOSKINS REACHED THE roof as MacIntyre used the flashlight to guide in the helicopter, which hovered fifty feet above her. He stayed on the ladder in case anything went wrong. MacIntyre used the high-powered flashlight to center the pilot over the roof and, when in the right position, signaled for him to land. As the helicopter descended, the downdraft blew two feet of accumulated snow in all directions, blinding Hoskins. He ducked back into the building. Snow fell through the opening on his head and shoulders.

The Seahawk rested its landing gear on the roof. MacIntyre ducked and ran to the port troop door, sliding it open.

"I'm glad to see you."

Alissa centered herself in the door and spoke loud enough

to be heard over the helicopter. "Not as happy as we are to see you."

Robson's voice coming through the headset interrupted the conversation. "We can't stay here long. The winds are too severe. We're going to head back to the airfield. Call us when you're ready."

Alissa gave the pilot a thumbs up. Removing her headset, she stepped aside so Boyce and Ken could jump out.

Chris hobbled over to the door. "Be careful out there. Don't get yourself killed."

"I'll do my best." Alissa leaned in and kissed him.

Chris closed the door and made his way back to his seat. The others crouched as the helicopter lifted off the roof and flew away to the north.

Hoskins re-emerged onto the roof. "Get inside where it's warm."

MacIntyre led the others to the opening and helped them down the ladder, following last and pulling the door closed behind her. Hoskins met them at the bottom, motioning for them to be quiet. Alissa could hear the deaders on the first floor churned into a frenzy by all the commotion above them. He ushered them down the corridor to where the other survivors were gathered.

As MacIntyre closed the door behind them, Hoskins stepped up to Alissa and offered his hand. "I'm Lieutenant Hoskins of the Maine National Guard."

"Alissa Madison."

After all the introductions had been made, Hoskins turned to Alissa. "Do you mind telling me what's going on? Why did the helicopter leave?"

"Leave?" Susie turned to Patricia. "I thought they were here to save us."

"They are." Patricia hugged the girl and glanced over at Alissa. "Right?"

Alissa made her way over to Susie and knelt in front of her.

"Of course, we'll get you out of here. But it'll take a little time."

"That still doesn't answer my question," said Hoskins.

Alissa positioned herself so she could see everyone in the room. "We're on a rescue mission to see if certain people survived at the hospital. We landed here because it was the only building with a flat roof. Don't worry. We'll get you out as well."

"We're in radio contact with two groups of survivors, one near the dock and the one at the hospital."

"Who's alive at the hospital?"

"Three of our men, a woman, a teenager, and that special patient who came in a few days ago."

"Do you know their names?" Alissa grew excited. "The woman and the teenager."

"I don't remember." Hoskins turned to MacIntyre. "Do you?"

"The woman is Roberta or Rebecca. She had a dog with her. The teenager is Kiera."

Alissa fell onto the cot and cried. Thank God, the others were alive. The uncertainty and anxiety dissipated. She hadn't gotten them killed after all.

Susie slid across the mattress and hugged her. "It's okay, lady. Now that you're here, we'll be fine."

Alissa sniffed back her tears and wiped her eyes with her left hand. With her right, she hugged Susie and kissed her on the forehead. She stood up and stepped over to Hoskins, removing the hand-drawn map from her jacket pocket and handing it to the lieutenant.

"You said there were two groups of survivors. Where is the second?"

Hoskins studied the map before pointing to the tip of a small peninsula to the northeast of their current position. "They're right here near the ferry. Captain Saunders, who is wounded, and Private Ames."

"That's good. We can pick them up after the hospital. How

far is the ferry dock from the hospital?"

"Another five or six miles," said Ken.

"Shit. That's a hell of a long way to walk in the middle of a blizzard."

"We might be able to help you with that." Hoskins smiled and motioned for Alissa to join him at the window. When she did, he pointed to the school bus parked outside. "We added the plow just before the storm and made sure she's gassed up. If we can get to her, we won't have to walk to the hospital and the ferry."

"What do you mean 'if we can get to her'?"

Alissa answered her own question when she saw the pack of deaders wandering around the bus.

"In addition to those, we have God knows how many more on the first floor."

"Can they get up here?" asked Boyce.

MacIntyre shook her head. "We blocked all the stairwells with furniture. There is no way anything is getting up here."

"Which also means there's no way of us getting down," added the lieutenant.

"We'll figure a way out. But first…." Alissa pointed to the radio. "…can I talk with Kiera?"

IT TOOK ROGERS several attempts to reach Hoskins. At first, he feared the worst until the lieutenant finally came on the air.

"Jesus, sir. You had me worried."

"Sorry. We were greeting our guests."

"So, you know about the helicopter that flew over the island?"

"It landed here a few minutes ago."

"Did it bring an extraction team?" Rogers asked excitedly.

"It's only Boyce and two civilians. They came to see if the vaccine patient is still alive."

"That figures." Rogers glanced up at the bathroom door leading into the hospital room. That patient and the civilians who accompanied him had been pains in the ass ever since they arrived on the island.

"It'll be okay. The few survivors who made it off the island are at Belfast Airport. Once we gather the survivors still on the island, the helicopter will fly us off, even if takes a few trips."

"Good to know."

"Tell the sergeant we'll contact him once we have a plan of action. In the meantime, pass the radio to Kyla." A voice in the background corrected Hoskins. "I mean Kiera."

"Sure thing."

Rogers cautiously opened the bathroom door and waved for Kiera. "Someone wants to talk to you," he whispered.

"Who?"

"I don't know."

Rogers briefed Costas as Kiera entered the bathroom. Shithead wagged his tail. Kiera crouched and leaned back against the wall, scratching the dog behind his ears as she raised the radio.

"This is Kiera."

"Kiera, hon. It's me. Alissa."

"Alissa!" Kiera almost yelled it. "You're alive?"

"Chris and I were the only ones to make it out of Boston."

"Where are you now?"

"Here on Warren Island. We're at the school."

"You've come to rescue us?"

"We're going to try. How is everyone else?"

"Rebecca and Shithead are here with me."

"And Nathan?"

"No change, but I guess that's a good thing." Kiera fought back a tear. "I'm so sorry for getting mad at you before you went into Boston."

"Don't worry about that now. You sit tight. We're coming to get you out."

"Good luck. This island is swarming with deaders."

"Don't worry. We have that covered."

"DO EITHER OF you see the airfield?" Robson asked over the intercom.

"We can barely see twenty feet in front of us," answered Frank.

Chris did not bother to reply. He moved from one side of the flight deck to the other as he searched for the landing strip. Despite it being day, the blizzard had covered everything on the island, making it difficult to distinguish anything other than structures. Nor did it help that the wind had increased, blowing the snow around and further limiting vision.

The wind let up for a minute. Chris spotted a two-thousand-foot-long strip stretching through the woods with two small buildings at the northern end.

"I see it off to our left. About two hundred feet away."

Frank leaned forward and gazed out the cockpit's side windshield. "He's right. We almost flew past it."

"We're going to get ourselves killed if we keep this up." Robson mumbled it to himself, but it came through loud and clear over the speakers in their headsets.

Robson maneuvered the Seahawk so he approached the airfield from the southeast, keeping the wind behind them, and hovered over the portion containing the terminal and tarmac, which offered him more landing space. He descended to an altitude of one hundred feet and stopped.

"Check the ground beneath us. I don't want to land on something buried in the snow."

Frank searched the area in front of the helicopter. "I don't see anything."

"Chris?"

"Hang on." He scanned the area beneath their right flank,

then moved over to port and did the same. "Nothing down there I can see."

"Any deaders?"

"I doubt they can make their way through this shit."

"I'll take what I can get. Make sure you're strapped in. This will be bumpy."

Chris buckled himself in near the starboard door so he could observe the landing.

Robson brought down the Seahawk slowly. The closer the helicopter got to the ground, the more snow that was churned up by the downdraft. Chris could tell they were about fifteen feet from the ground. He realized he had been holding his breath and exhaled with—

The wind picked up suddenly. A downdraft combined with a crosswind slammed into the Seahawk. The landing gear absorbed the shock and bounced the helicopter a few feet back into the air where the wind tipped it to port at a fifteen-degree angle. The tips of the rotors slashed through the snow and clipped the concrete beneath. The rending of metal filled the troop compartment as all four rotors were torn from the engine, breaking into pieces, the shards hurtling across the airfield, one crashing through the window of the main terminal. The helicopter's fuselage rolled and teetered a moment before coming to a rest on its port side. A few seconds later, the engines ground to a halt and a deadly silence fell over the airfield.

Chapter Six

I T TOOK THIRTY minutes to develop a plan to rescue the stranded survivors and coordinate it among all three groups. It suffered from several disadvantages, mostly involving a handful of humans, half of them civilians, battling two thousand of the living dead in the middle of a blizzard that severely limited their ability to move. Add to that the groups had few weapons and limited ammunition and the odds of success, despite the bravado, did not appear all that good.

The school group spent five minutes gathering everything they needed, including winter boots, a parka, and gloves for Alissa. For weapons, they had four carbines and four Sig Sauers between them, each with an average of three magazines of ammunition, and the only suppressor being on Alissa's sidearm. In addition to the Ka-Bar knife Alissa carried and the one Chris gave to Boyce, the group scrounged up from the abandoned personal possessions two hunting knives, one switchblade, a baseball bat with a six-inch steel spike drilled through the end, as well as a Glock 23 .40 caliber semiautomatic pistol, a 9mm Makarov semiautomatic pistol, each with an extra magazine, and an old .38 caliber revolver. The weapons were evenly distributed among the group with everyone except Susie receiving a way to defend themselves.

Alissa, Hoskins, MacIntyre, and Boyce checked out the elevator halfway down the corridor. Using a crowbar found in the supply closet, Alissa pried open the doors so MacIntyre and Boyce could push them aside. Thankfully, the elevator sat on the first floor or their plan would have to be scrapped.

"So far so good," said Hoskins. "Let's check out stage two."

Boyce used a broom from the janitor's closest with a coat hanger duct taped to one end to hook the elevator cables and pull them toward the opening. Hoskins grabbed them and swung out into the shaft, lowering himself to the roof of the car. Kneeling, he rapped on it once. Nothing happened. Lifting the access panel, he crouched and peered inside. It was empty.

Hoskins gave a thumbs up.

Using the same procedure, Boyce, Patricia, Ramirez, and Ken joined them. Alissa and MacIntyre lowered Susie to the others.

"Are you okay?" asked Alissa.

MacIntyre nodded. "Just hurry up and clear a path for me. I don't know how long I can contain them. When that horn blares, all hell is going to break loose."

"Good luck."

MacIntyre used the broom to pull the cable closer for Alissa to slide down. Hoskins and Boyce had lowered themselves into the elevator. Alissa joined them.

Hoskins held the crowbar in his hand. "Okay, ladies and gentlemen," he whispered. "It's showtime."

MACINTYRE STROLLED TO the stairwell at the northern end of the school. During the initial attack, they had pushed school chairs, cots, and any furniture that could be found down the twin stairwells to block the rampaging deaders. It worked. The structural integrity of those barricades would now be put to the test.

Centering herself at the top of the stairwell, MacIntyre withdrew her Sig Sauer.

"Hey, meat sacks!"

The four deaders on the landing spun around to face Mac-Intyre. She fired a single round into the face of the closest deader, an elderly woman whose dentures had fallen out. Its head exploded, showering the others behind it in gore. The action had the desired effect. The noise, the violence, and the smell of fresh meat incited the deaders into a frenzy. The other three charged MacIntyre, attempting to crawl over the pile of furniture to get her. Carnage broke out on the first floor as every deader in the building rushed to the commotion. The pack ran up the stairs, crashing into the makeshift barricade. It moved a few inches. For a moment, MacIntyre thought the deaders would break through and overwhelm her. The pile of furniture compacted and held. Deaders tried to scale it, becoming entangled in the metal arms and legs.

Hurry up, you guys, she thought.

INSIDE THE ELEVATOR, Alissa and the others heard the gunshot followed by the stampede of the deaders to the stairwell, waiting until the pack was at the other end of the building trying to reach MacIntyre.

Hoskins snapped his fingers and pointed to the doors.

Boyce moved forward, inserted the crowbar between the twin sliding doors, and pried them open a few inches. Nothing moved on the other side. Hoskins raised his carbine into the low-ready position, moved to the center of the car, and nodded. Alissa and Boyce pulled them open enough for someone to slip through. Boyce raised his weapon and he and Hoskins passed through into the corridor, each scanning the southern and northern sectors, respectively. No deaders were in sight. Hoskins looked at Alissa, pumped his left fist up and down by his head, then raised his forefinger to his lips.

Alissa stepped beneath the access panel and whispered, "Now."

Ramirez lowered himself into the elevator, then helped Ken lower Patricia and Susie inside. Ken joined them last. Boyce motioned for them to follow. Slowly and quietly, the group made its way to the school's southern exit, Boyce and Alissa in the lead, Ramirez and Ken on either side of the women, and Hoskins bringing up the rear.

At the end of the corridor, everyone formed a line. When Hoskins nodded, Boyce opened the door and stepped out onto the landing. The stairs turned left and ran adjacent to the building. Boyce descended, scanning the area in front of him. Ken and Alissa moved out onto the landing, scanning the northern and eastern flanks. Once certain there were no deaders around, Alissa waved for the others to join them, whispering for the civilians to follow Boyce. Hoskins brought up the rear, unlocking the door from the outside so he could gain access to the building, then shutting it quietly.

Boyce stopped at the corner of the building and peered around back. Four deaders stood by the school bus, each covered in a few inches of snow and showing little movement. He knew at least twice that many were on the other side of the bus or just out of sight. Hoskins and Alissa joined him.

"We have four between us and the bus, plus another four to six in the area," the medic advised.

"We can't risk gunfire," said Hoskins. "If those things in the stairwell come running, they'll trap MacIntyre inside."

Alissa tapped her Ka-Bar. "What about knifing them?"

"Are you up to it?"

"Wouldn't be the first time."

Hoskins turned to Ken and pointed to his carbine. "You know how to use that?"

"Did some time in Africa and the Middle East."

"Excellent. You and Ramirez protect the women. We're going to take out those deaders silently. Don't fire your weapons unless absolutely necessary."

"Roger that."

Turning to Alissa and Boyce, he ordered, "Let's go."

The three slung their carbines over their shoulders, removed their bladed weapons, and rounded the corner.

WHAT IS TAKING so long? thought MacIntyre. She checked her watch. Damn, it had only been seven minutes. It seemed like an hour. She had to keep them occupied a little longer.

Jumping onto her end of the barricade, MacIntyre growled at the deaders, sending them into a frenzy.

ALISSA APPROACHED FROM the rear the closest deader, a male dressed in a blood-soaked National Guard uniform and with the right side of its face eaten off. Moving through two feet of snow proved more difficult than originally thought. Doing so quietly was damn near impossible. For some reason, the deader had not noticed her. Alissa curled and uncurled her fingers around the handle of the Ka-Bar to keep them from freezing.

When six feet away, the Guardsman deader turned to Alissa. It didn't snarl, didn't lunge. In fact, it seemed oblivious of her. Alissa pushed through the snow, used her left hand to grab it by the collar, and plunged the Ka-Bar through its right eye. She angled the blade down into its limbic system and twisted. The thing barely responded, stiffening for a second before collapsing, pulling itself off the blade.

The muffled sound of the body hitting the snow attracted the attention of the other three deaders. Alissa expected them to attack, raising the alarm for the others. Instead, they shuffled through the accumulation toward the humans. Alissa, Hoskins, and Boyce made their way toward them, stopping a few feet away and waiting for the deaders to get closer, then dispatching them with a knife blow to the head.

With the visible threats removed, they headed to the back of the school bus. Hoskins checked the right flank. Three deaders stood between them and the front door. The lieutenant held up his thumb and two fingers, warning the others what they faced.

Boyce pointed to himself and Hoskins, then to the rear of the bus, running his forefinger in a three-sided square to indicate the rear emergency door. Hoskins replied with the okay signal then leaned over to whisper to Alissa.

"We're going to clear the bus. Cover us."

Alissa nodded.

Boyce grabbed the exterior handle to the rear emergency door, waited for Hoskins to acknowledge he was ready, then opened it. No pack of deaders flowed out. The lieutenant climbed in, checked the last three rows for deaders, then helped Boyce inside. Both men made their way to the front. Nothing was aboard the bus.

Boyce slid into the driver's seat. "The keys are in the ignition."

"Can you drive one of these?"

"It shouldn't be difficult. Do you want me to start it?"

"Let's get the civilians on board first."

Hoskins made his way to the back and jumped out. Alissa kept her attention focused on the three deaders beside the vehicle. He tapped her on the shoulder.

"I'm going to get the others. Wait here and help them on, then have Boyce start the bus and honk the horn three times."

"Where are you going?"

"To cover MacIntyre's escape." Hoskins rushed off to the end of the school.

"Is everything okay?" asked Patricia.

"Everything is fine. Head over to the bus and get inside. Alissa will help you. I'll follow in a minute."

The four civilians headed for the bus, following the tracks in the snow made by the others. As they approached, Alissa held her forefinger against her lips, telling them to stay quiet.

"I'm cold," whispered Susie.

"We'll turn on the heat once we start the engine." Alissa lifted Susie onto the bus. "Take a seat near the front."

Patricia climbed on board followed by Ramirez and Ken. Ramirez made his way to the front.

"If you want, I'll take over. I used to drive one of these

part-time."

"Be my guest." Boyce changed places with Ramirez.

Ramirez turned the ignition. The engine emitted a half roar and died.

The three deaders beside the bus raised their heads.

"Shit," mumbled Boyce. "Is the battery dead?"

"That would be a clicking noise. I got this." Ramirez pumped the gas pedal three times and tried it again. This time, the engine started, blowing a cloud of black smoke out the exhaust, covering Alissa. She choked and hacked.

"Hit the horn three times," ordered Boyce.

Ramirez did, sending the signal to MacIntyre.

MACINTYRE CHECKED HER watch again. She had been at the barricade seventeen minutes, growing nervous that something had—

Three blares from the bus horn sounded outside. About fucking time.

The deaders farthest from the barricade turned their attention to the new potential source of food.

MacIntyre shouldered her carbine, unsheathed her knife, and sliced the blade along her left thumb. Squeezing the base, she dripped blood on the barricade. The smell had the desired effect. Most of the deaders were driven into a frenzy and attacked. Some that seemed more intelligent than the others began pulling away the furniture to get at her. MacIntyre unslung her carbine and fired into the pack, taking down three and wounding several others. The damage had been done, however. The weakened structure gave way under the onslaught and fell apart, furniture cascading down the stairs. Seven deaders broke through and lunged toward her.

MacIntyre ran to the elevator.

She had no way of knowing that the last seven deaders in the pack had reversed direction and rushed back to the first floor.

ALISSA JUMPED BACK from the bus to escape the exhaust. Noticing her, the three deaders lurched toward her, their pace slowed by the accumulated snow. *No sense in being quiet now*, thought Alissa. Raising her carbine, she took them down with shots to the head.

Boyce popped his head through the emergency exit. "Is everything okay?"

"Just clearing the area."

No one on the bus noticed the seven deaders at the other end of the building, attracted by the noise, making their way through the storm toward them.

HOSKINS WATCHED AS the seven deaders raced onto the first floor, searching for food. He raised his carbine, aimed, and took down two with single shots to their heads.

Spotting prey, the other five charged.

MACINTYRE RAN DOWN the hall and jumped into elevator shaft, grabbed the cables, and slid down to the roof. As she lowered herself through the panel, five deaders rushed through the open doors above her, raining down on the elevator. To prevent from being crushed, she dropped into the car, twisting her ankle when she hit. A female deader in street clothes fell in after her while a deader in a National Guard uniform crawled through the panel. Both glared at her and snarled.

MacIntyre removed her Sig Sauer from its holster and fired three rounds into the head of the female deader, throwing it against the opposite wall. She shifted her aim and took out the one dangling from the ceiling with a single shot. Blood dripped from its shattered head. Using the handrail attached to the wall, she lifted herself to her feet. Above her, more deaders landed on the roof.

Outside the elevator, the five remaining deaders switched their attention from Hoskins and stormed the partially opened door. A deader with no right arm pushed its way through. MacIntyre placed the barrel of the Sig Sauer against its forehead and fired, blasting off the top of its skull and covering her in gore. The limbic system remained intact so the deader still attempted to get at her. She aimed through the ruptured skull and fired, blowing off the rest of its head. As the body slid to the floor, two more deaders attempted to crawl over it.

A loud thump landed behind her. MacIntyre spun around. A third deader had pushed the Guardsman through the panel and attempted to climb down. MacIntyre aimed and fired two rounds through its skull. The deader went limp.

A hand clutched her shoulder. One of the deaders pushing through the elevator doors had grabbed her. MacIntyre spun around, using her gun hand to break its grip, and jumped into the far corner. The deader collapsed into the elevator and struggled to its feet. MacIntyre fired two shots into its temple, then switched her aim and took down the third deader blocking her escape with two more shots. Two more living dead faces centered themselves in the opening. MacIntyre switched out magazines and fired two rounds into each of them. With no more deaders outside, she began pulling away the bodies.

Another thud sounded from behind her. The pack above had pushed the corpse through the panel and two more had jumped down. MacIntyre fired one round into each of their heads, bringing them down, then double tapped them. Another dropped down, tripping on the bodies and falling to the side. She placed a round through its gaping mouth.

"Give me your hand."

MacIntyre glanced over her shoulder. Hoskins stood in the corridor, reaching through the open doors. She reached out her left hand. The lieutenant grabbed it and pulled her to safety over the pile of bodies.

A teenage girl deader dropped through the panel and rushed MacIntyre, landing on her right leg. Being halfway through the doors, she had no room to aim. The teenage deader sunk its teeth into MacIntyre's right thigh, ripping through her uniform and tearing into skin. MacIntyre cried out in agony. Once in the corridor, she lowered her Sig Sauer and emptied her magazine into its head.

Hoskins tried to help her up. "Let's get out of here."

"It's too late for that." MacIntyre unslung her carbine and handed it and her pouch of ammunition to the lieutenant, then reloaded her Sig Sauer. "I'll hold them off so you can get to safety."

Three more deaders fell into the elevator and charged the opening. MacIntyre took down the first with a single round to the head, slowing the other two. More entered the elevator.

"Go!" she snapped.

Hoskins saluted and took off down the corridor.

MacIntyre kept firing on the deaders until she ran out of ammunition. As she changed magazines, three deaders surged through the elevator doors and attacked, feeding on her left leg and arms.

HOSKINS REACHED THE end of the corridor when he heard MacIntyre scream amidst the feeding frenzy. He turned in time to see three deaders ravaging her. Taking aim, the lieutenant fired two rounds into MacIntyre's head, putting the soldier out of her misery.

The gunfire caught the deaders' attention. As one, they turned toward Hoskins and charged. The lieutenant emptied his magazine into them and bolted out the emergency exit. As he rounded the building, switching out cartridges as he ran, he heard the door slam open and the pack charge after him. This one would be close.

ALISSA SAW HOSKINS race around the corner of the building.

"They're almost here," she yelled to Ramirez.

Boyce stood above her, centered in the emergency exit. "Where's MacIntyre?"

Hoskins waved for Alissa to get into the bus. She wondered why until four deaders circled the corner in pursuit of the lieutenant.

Boyce could not fire without risking hitting Hoskins. Alissa took five steps to the left, aimed her carbine at the closest deader, and fired a single shot. The round took it down. She switched to the next closest, killing it with two rounds.

By now, Hoskins had gotten close enough to the bus that Boyce could bring down the last two.

"Where's MacIntyre?" he asked.

"She didn't make it." Hoskins jumped into the back of the bus. "Alissa, get in here. Now."

Before she could ask why, three more deaders rounded the corner of the school. Hoskins and Boyce each took a hand and lifted her on board a second before the pack reached the bus. A deader in a sheriff deputy's uniform tried to crawl in. Alissa kicked it in the face, propelling it backward and knocking over the others. Boyce used the opportunity to close and secure the emergency exit.

Two more deaders raced around the corner.

Hoskins headed for the front of the bus. "Let's go."

"No complaints here." Ramirez shifted into drive and pressed his foot on the accelerator.

The rear wheels spun, unable to gain traction in the snow.

Chapter Seven

"**I** THOUGHT THIS fucking thing had a plow," snapped Hoskins.

"It does." Ramirez remained calm. "But a plow isn't going to do anything for the two feet of snow that collected around the tires."

As they talked, the five deaders from inside the school, joined by two more, descended on the bus. They snarled and scratched at the windows, desperate to get at the food inside.

Alissa lowered one of the side windows to shoot at them, but Boyce stopped her.

"Don't waste your ammo."

Ramirez shifted into reverse and gunned the engine, forcing the bus backward into the snow. It moved a few inches before stopping. Ramirez shifted into drive and gunned the engine a second time. The bus lurched forward, gaining a little momentum. He continued the rocking motion.

"What's that?" asked Ken, who stood behind the driver's seat.

"Where?"

"Up ahead of us."

Hoskins reached down and flicked on the bus's headlights. The beam fell upon eight snow-encrusted deaders pushing through the storm toward them.

"Calm down," Ramirez grinned. "I got this."

On the fourth rock forward, the rear tires gained traction and moved forward three feet. Once off the compacted snow, the vehicle lurched forward and gained speed. The deaders along the side ran with it, frantic to keep up. Most slipped, a couple falling under the bus where the wheels ran over them. Ramirez had accelerated to fifteen miles an hour when the blades of the plow hit the deaders in front of them, not enough to kill or immobilize them, only shove them out of the way. At the end of the building, Ramirez maneuvered around to the front parking lot, accelerated through onto the access road leading off the grounds, and turned left onto Pendleton Point Road.

Alissa made her way to the rear of the vehicle and looked out. She knew the deaders were following, but Ramirez had put enough distance between them that the living dead would find it difficult to follow them. She made her way to the front of the bus.

As Alissa passed by Susie, the little girl tugged on her coat sleeve. "Aunt Alissa?"

"Yes?" She crouched to be at eye level with her.

"Thank you for saving us."

"You're welcome." Alissa cupped Susie's cheek in her hand. "But we have to rescue a few more people before we can get off this island. Is that okay?"

Susie smiled bravely and nodded. Alissa kissed her on the forehead and continued to the front of the bus.

"How much longer?" Hoskins asked Ramirez.

"The hospital is two miles up this road."

"Good. I'll let Costas know we're on our way."

As Hoskins moved to the rear to contact the hospital, Boyce tapped Alissa on the arm. "Did you notice something strange about those deaders outside the school?"

"You mean moving so slow?"

"They were all runners when they reached the school yesterday," said Ramirez.

"I think we found a secret weapon against them." Ken smiled. "They can't function in cold."

"Neither can I." Ramirez chuckled. "I wanted to retire in Florida."

"You might get your chance," said Alissa. "If the snow and cold immobilizes those things, we stand a chance of getting off this island alive."

SAUNDERS JARRED HIMSELF awake from a nap. He reached for his weapon, realizing he did not need it.

"Are you okay, sir?" asked Ames.

The captain shifted in his chair to relieve the pressure on his rear. "My leg's killing me, and it's as cold as Hell in here."

"I doubt it's very cold in Hell," responded Ames good-naturedly.

"It doesn't matter. I'd rather be there than here."

"Soon enough, sir."

"I hope so. How long has it been since we last heard from the retrieval team?"

"It hasn't been an hour yet."

"Shit." Saunders glanced out the windows. "Any signs of deaders?"

"Nothing. But this storm is so thick, they could be ten feet out and I wouldn't see them."

Saunders stood, groaning when he put pressure on his wounded leg. It felt numb, almost as if it were asleep. He limped around, trying to get the blood flowing.

"Let's hope that damn bus gets here soon."

CONSCIOUSNESS CAME SLOWLY to Chris. He recalled a gust of wind tilting the helicopter to one side and the resulting accident. He didn't feel fire around him, so the helicopter hadn't burst into flames during the crash and he hadn't died. Yet.

He felt himself suspended in mid-air with something pushing against his chest and thighs. For a moment, his addled brain couldn't figure out where he was. When Chris opened his eyes, he realized he still sat in his seat near the starboard door of the Seahawk, only the helicopter lay on its port side and he hovered ten feet in the air.

"Good. You're alive." Robson had unbuckled himself and checked on the co-pilot.

"I'm beginning to think nothing can kill me. I'll come through the apocalypse being physically worn away bit by bit." Chris reached for his seatbelt catch.

"Hang on. I'll help you down in a minute."

"Okay." Chris motioned toward the co-pilot. "How's Frank?"

"He didn't make it. The crash snapped his neck."

"I'm sorry."

Robson said a silent prayer over his fallen comrade. "At least he died doing what he loved."

Robson made his way out of the cockpit and into the main troop compartment, being careful not to twist his ankle on the debris littering the area. He centered himself beneath Chris, made sure he had good footing, and wrapped his arms around Chris' legs.

"Unbuckle yourself and hold on to your seat. I'll help lower you down."

It took two awkward minutes to get Chris from his perch. If Robson had been Alissa, Chris might have enjoyed it more. Once safely on solid ground, Robson let go. Chris leaned against the rear wall, supporting himself on his good leg. The bandages over the wound in his right leg felt moist and a trickle of blood ran down his skin.

"How bad is it?" Robson pointed to Chris' leg.

"I think the stitches came undone. I'll live."

"Good." Robson smiled. "This mission has ruined my ac-creditation as a pilot."

"Don't worry. I'll give you a five-star review on Yelp."

"You know what they say. If you can walk away from one

of my landings—"

"—it's a miracle."

Both men laughed, breaking the tension.

"Should we call the others and let them know we're down for the count?"

"Can't. The radio got trashed in the crash. I have no way to contact them."

"Which means they don't know we're out of commission."

"Exactly." Robson leaned against the pilot's chair. "We're safe for now. We're protected from the elements and I don't smell aviation fuel, so we're in no danger of catching on fire. The others know we were heading to the airfield, so we sit tight until they come for us."

"If they come for us."

"From what I've seen of your friend Alissa, she won't leave us behind."

Chris nodded, though a part of him wondered if once she had rescued Nathan would he become her only priority.

"WE HAVE A problem," said Ramirez.

Alissa and Hoskins joined him.

"What's wrong?" asked the lieutenant.

Ramirez pointed ahead of the bus. The weight of the snow had snapped a dead tree and it now lay across the road, blocking their path.

"Can we push it out of the way?" asked Alissa.

"Maybe if I could push one end aside, but the center is across the road."

"Can we take another route?"

Ramirez shook his head. "This is the only way."

"How far are we from the hospital?" asked Hoskins.

"A quarter of a mile, maybe less."

"Then we walk from here."

"All of us?" Patricia grew alarmed.

"No. Just me, Alissa, and Ken. The rest of you stay here. Ramirez and Boyce, protect the women." Hoskins handed Ramirez MacIntyre's carbine and a spare magazine. "Have you ever shot one of these?"

"I've shot a hunting rifle."

"Close enough."

"What about me?" asked Patricia.

The lieutenant handed her the Glock 23.

Patricia looked over the sidearm. "Where's the safety?"

"The safety's in the trigger. All you have to do is aim and shoot."

The woman nodded her understanding.

Alissa knelt on the seat in front of Susie and held her hands. "Don't worry, hon. We'll come back for you."

"I know you will. I trust you." Susie stood and kissed Alissa on the cheek.

Hoskins tapped Ramirez on the shoulder. "Where is the hospital from here?"

"The Baptist church and the Post Office are up ahead. The hospital is a quarter of a mile beyond that on the left. You can't miss it."

"Thanks." Hoskins turned to the others. "Let's go."

Ramirez opened the side door and the three set off in the blizzard up the main road.

COSTAS CALLED EVERYONE into the bathroom to brief them. It was cramped, but at least they could talk without drawing attention from the deaders outside the room.

"Hoskins is on his way to get us out of here. We have to be ready to go once they arrive."

"What about Nathan?" asked Rebecca. "He's still unconscious."

"I can carry him," said Costas. "What are the chances of him turning."

"If he hasn't by now, I doubt he will," offered Kiera.

"That's good enough for me."

"Is there any way we can put a muzzle on the dog?" asked Murphy. "If he starts barking, he'll bring the deaders down on us."

Rebecca thought for a moment. "I can wrap gauze around his mouth."

Kiera chuckled. "Good luck with that. He's not going to like it."

"He'll have to put up with it until we get to the bus."

EVEN THOUGH ONLY a quarter of a mile, it seemed like a twenty-mile hike between the cold, trudging through two-and-a-half feet of snow, and the wind blowing in their faces. If Alissa made it through the outbreak, she promised herself she would retire to the southwest.

Eventually, they reached the hospital. From the corner of the road, they checked out the grounds. Four cars sat parked out by the main entrance, snow-covered mounds in the otherwise flat surface. Two National Guard Humvees stood behind the cars, their doors open. An ambulance sat at the outer edge of the parking lot adjacent to the road. At least a dozen deaders filled the parking lot, immobile and covered in snow like at the school.

"At least they're not runners," said Ken.

Hoskins shook his head. "They still pose a threat when we try to get into the hospital. There are too many for the three of us to take down with knives, and I don't want to waste ammo on them. We're limited as it is."

Alissa shivered. "What are we going to do?"

"I have an idea. Follow me."

Hoskins backed into the woods ten feet, moved along the tree line until the ambulance blocked his view of the deaders, then cut back across the road. When they reached the ambulance, the lieutenant gently rapped on the exterior. Nothing responded from inside. Moving around to the rear of the vehicle, he raised his carbine and motioned for Alissa to open the doors. She did.

The ambulance was empty.

Alissa and Ken climbed in. After scanning the deaders in the parking lot to make certain they had not been noticed, Hoskins joined them and quietly closed the doors behind him.

"It's nice to get out of the storm," said Ken.

"Enjoy it while it lasts. It'll only be for a few minutes." Hoskins rummaged through the bins.

"There are too many deaders out front to enter through there, and my guess is the lobby and first floor are swarming with them."

Alissa rubbed her hands together, trying to get the blood flowing. "Our best bet is to go in through the emergency exit on the left end of the building."

"I agree." Hoskins withdrew a bottle of alcohol and placed it on the floor. "Which room is your friend located in?"

"Second floor, front left corner."

"According to Costas, there's a pack of deaders on the second floor we'll have to contend with, as well as what's on the first floor." Hoskins moved over to the stretcher and pulled the case off the pillow.

"Does he know how many?" asked Ken.

"He's not sure. At least six to eight."

Alissa shifted on the stretcher. "Tough, but doable."

"I'm worried about the ammo situation. Depending on how many there are on the first floor, we're going to use a lot clearing them out."

Hoskins doused one end of the pillowcase in alcohol and laid it on the floor. "Does anyone have a lighter or matches?"

"I gave up smoking years ago," said Ken.

"What are you doing?" asked Alissa.

"Taking care of the deaders in the parking lot."

Hoskins moved to the driver's portion of the ambulance and searched the seats and dashboard. He opened the glove compartment and withdrew a pack of Camel cigarettes with a lighter wedged between the cardboard and the plastic wrapper. He removed it. "Thank God for bad habits."

Alissa and Ken stared at each, confused.

Hoskins crouched and removed the radio from his pocket. "Costas, can you hear me?"

"Loud and clear. Where are you?"

"In the parking lot. We're coming in to get you in a minute. Move when you get the signal."

"What signal?"

Hoskins smiled. "Trust me. You'll know it. See you in a few."

"Roger that. Good luck."

Hoskins slid the radio back into his pocket and turned to the others. "Circle around the parking lot so the deaders don't see you and head for the emergency entrance. I'll give you five minutes and then I'll join you."

Alissa opened the rear doors and stepped out. None of the deaders had moved. She motioned for Ken to follow and they trudged off through the snow. Hoskins crouched by the rear bumper, keeping an eye on the pack.

COSTAS HANDED THE radio to Murphy. "They'll be here in a few minutes."

The sergeant and Rogers untied Nathan's hands and legs from the bedpost, using the restraints to lace them together. Costas took a roll of gauze from the nightstand and wrapped it around Nathan's mouth.

"What about my weapons?" whispered Rogers.

"I'll take them," said Kiera.

Rogers glanced over at the sergeant for permission.

"Do you know how to use them?" asked Costas.

"No offense," said Rebecca. "But she's probably as good a shot as you."

Kiera grinned and nodded.

"They're yours."

Kiera took the Sig Sauer. "Is there a round in the chamber?"

"Of course."

She slid the weapon between her jeans and the small of her back, then took the carbine. She switched off the safety, made certain it was in semi-automatic mode, and stood by the door with the barrel aimed at the floor.

Costas looked at the other soldiers and nodded his approval.

They waited for the melee to begin.

ALISSA AND KEN approached the emergency entrance. Five deaders stood in the area, covered in snow and immobile like the ones out front. She shouldered her carbine and removed the Ka-Bar from its sheath. As Ken kept his weapon trained on them, Alissa snuck up behind the closest deader, a female in a National Guard uniform. If the deader heard, it gave no signs. Grabbing it by the back of the collar, she drove the blade between where the spine entered the skull and twirled the blade around. The deader stiffened and went limp. Alissa held it, allowing it to gently drop into the snow. She checked the pockets in its vest and found five magazines filled with 5.56mm rounds and two magazines for a Sig Sauer. She removed the vest and draped it over her shoulder.

Attracted by the noise, the other four, three wearing hospital scrubs and one in civilian clothes, turned toward her.

Ken raised his carbine.

Alissa shook her head. "I got this."

She removed her Sig Sauer and took them down with one round to each head, the suppressor muffling the sound. With the threat neutralized, they moved into position by the entrance.

HOSKINS CHECKED HIS watch. Four minutes had passed.

Moving to the left side of the ambulance, he removed the gas cap and shoved the pillowcase down the pipe, leaving only the alcohol-soaked tip exposed. He opened the driver's door, reached in, and switched on the siren and warning lights. The colors and sounds broke through the density of the blizzard. As anticipated, the deaders in the parking lot turned to the ambulance and shambled toward it.

Hoskins removed the lighter, flicked it on, and held the flame beneath the pillowcase. The material caught fire. Pocketing the lighter, he took off, following Alissa and Ken's footprints to the emergency entrance.

The flames reached the fuel tank at the same time as the deaders gathered around the ambulance. The explosion tore them apart, sending body parts and pieces of the ambulance across the area and into the street. The concussion set off two car alarms and blasted out the windows along the front of the building.

Inside the lobby, close to thirty runners milled about. They were driven into a frenzy by the explosion and raced to the front of the building. Being blocked by the cars parked out front, the glass doors suffered little damage from the blast. The horde surged against them until one of the deaders accidentally pressed against the power button. The twin doors swung open, allowing the horde to surge into the parking lot in search of food.

Chapter Eight

"WHAT WAS THAT?" asked Susie.

The others in the bus knew. They recognized the sound of an explosion and spotted the black mushroom cloud even through the storm.

Patricia hugged Susie. "Somebody is setting off fireworks."

"In a blizzard?" Susie crinkled her brows. "It sounded like something blew up."

Ramirez unsuccessfully tried to stifle a laugh. He tapped Boyce on the shoulder and gestured toward the back. "Kids today are a lot smarter than we were."

"What does that mean?" asked Susie.

Ramirez turned to the girl and smiled. "It means you were right. That was an explosion."

"Is that a good thing?"

"Yes, it is. It means Alissa and the others are killing dead-ers."

"DO YOU HEAR that?" Robson turned his head.

"What?"

"Sounds like sirens."

Chris listened for a moment. "I don't hear anything."

A minute later, a muffled explosion cut through the wind.

Chris pointed to the outside. "That I heard."

"That doesn't sound promising."

"At least they can't blame me this time."

Robson stared at him quizzically.

"I'll explain later."

"DID I JUST hear an explosion?" Saunders sat upright in the chair and leaned forward to glance out the window.

"It sounds like it came from the east."

"Where the other groups of survivors are." He removed the radio from his pocket. "I want to find out what's going on."

ALISSA, HOSKINS, AND Ken cautiously entered the emergency room through the bay door used for ambulances drop offs, their weapons in the low-ready position. The corridor extended for ten feet then turned right. Hoskins inched his way to the corner, stopped, and peered around the corner. Fourteen deaders scratched at the door at the other end of the emergency room, drawn by the noise out front. Most wore scrubs. Three were adorned in National Guard uniforms. One wore civilian clothes.

The lieutenant whispered to the others. "We can't go in this way. There's a pack of those things blocking the exit."

"We can try the visitor's entrance to the ER. We can access the main hospital—"

Saunders' voice boomed over the radio. "Hoskins, Murphy. Can you hear me. We heard an explosion. Is everything all right?"

Hoskins removed the radio and shut it off, but too late. The pack heard the noise, spun around, and rushed down the corridor.

"What do we do now?" asked Ken.

"We fight." Alissa moved around the corner and fired into

the pack.

"Shit." Hoskins joined her.

The first volley took down four deaders but failed to stop the others.

Ken spotted an empty stretcher against the wall. Running over to it, he pushed it ten feet down the corridor, swung it sideways so it blocked their path, and tipped it over. It only slowed the charge.

As Ken fell back, a female deader in blue scrubs leapt over the barricade, landing on and knocking him to the floor. Ken stopped it from lunging by shoving his left hand against its chin, the palm pushing it away. The deader snapped at his hand, aiming for the exposed flesh extending from his fingerless gloves. Ken twisted his hand to the side but not in time. It caught the pinky in his mouth and bit down.

"Fuck!"

Alissa raced up, placed the carbine against its jaw, and fired a round. The deader's head exploded, splattering blood and gore across the wall. As Ken backed away, a second deader in a National Guard uniform bound over the stretcher. Alissa jumped aside. The deader crashed face first on the floor. Alissa slammed the stock of her weapon into the back of its head four times before its skull collapsed, scattering brain matter across the floor.

Three deaders tripped over the stretcher and struggled to get back to their feet. Hoskins blasted the one in front of him but could not reach the two in front of Alissa without risking catching her in the crossfire. He continued picking off the pack on the other side of the stretcher, clearing them all.

Alissa did not have time to aim. She rammed the stock of the carbine against the first deader's face, knocking it back onto the stretcher. Swinging the weapon to her left, she fractured the skull of the second deader, dropping it to the floor. A shot rang out from behind her. The second deader's head exploded. Alissa glanced over her shoulder. Ken lay against the wall, the carbine in his hands, and gave her a thumbs up. Spinning around again, she battered the head of the first deader until it no longer moved.

An eerie silence fell over the emergency room, punctuated by Ken's crying.

Alissa ran over and knelt beside him. "I'm sorry you were bit."

"I never expected to make it out of here alive." Ken wiped the tears from his eyes with his uninjured hand. "The deader that attacked me was my daughter. She worked here at the hospital."

Alissa hugged him. What else could she do?

Hoskins stood in front of them. "Do you want me to put you out of your misery?"

"No." Ken sniffed back his tears and stood. "It'll be a few minutes before I turn. I can still be of help."

"Good man. Thanks." Hoskins headed outside toward the visitor's entrance.

Ken followed.

Alissa brought up the rear, prepared to mercy Ken when the time came.

THE GUNFIRE ECHOING from the first floor told those trapped in the room that help had arrived.

Kiera moved over to the phone on the side of the bed and lifted the receiver.

"What are you doing?" asked Murphy.

"Watch."

She scanned the buttons and pressed one. The phone at the nurses' station began to ring. Snarling and the stamping of feet came from the corridor as the deaders descended on the station.

Murphy cocked an eyebrow. "Smart girl."

"Thanks." Kiera placed the handset on the nightstand.

Murphy moved to the door and turned to the others. "Anyone up for kicking some deader ass?"

Costas joined him.

Kiera stepped up and readied her carbine. "I'm here to chew bubblegum and kick ass, and I'm all out of bubble gum."

Costas chuckled, getting the reference.

Murphy opened the door and the three of them stepped into the corridor.

RELIEVED TO FIND no deaders in the ER waiting room, the group made its way to the double doors leading to the rest of the building. Hoskins peered through the glass panes. No deaders could be seen.

"It looks like my diversion worked," he said. "Let's go."

Ken moved in front of the lieutenant. "Let me go first. I'm expendable."

With Ken in the lead, the three entered the main part of the building.

THIRTEEN DEADERS HOVERED around the nurses' station, clutching at the ringing phone. Distracted, none of them were aware of the humans until a hail of bullets rained down upon them.

Five fell with the first barrage. The others turned and rushed the humans, becoming engulfed in gunfire. None got to within ten feet of their prey. As Kiera stayed behind to protect their rear, Murphy and Costas moved forward, double tapping any deader that still moved and making sure the rest of the corridor was clear. Once certain they had cleared any danger, the Guardsmen fell back to the room and took up position outside the door.

Murphy leaned inside. "Our ride should be here shortly."

KEN REACHED THE lobby and motioned for the others to halt. He scanned the area, moved over to the receptionist desk, and looked through the Plexiglas divider. A female deader, its face chewed off, popped up and attacked, hitting the divider. It snarled and snapped at Ken but could not get to him, instead smearing blood and pieces of tissue across the surface. Being locked in its area, it posed no threat. Ken gave it the finger and joined the others.

"Well?" asked Hoskins.

"It's clear. We—"

Gunfire from the second floor interrupted him. The three spun around to face the stairwell diagonal from the receptionist area, their weapons raised, expecting to be swarmed. After a moment, the gunfire ceased.

"Come on." Ken led the way. He paused at the landing, peered around the corner, and waved the others on. They stopped at the top of the stairs. A pile of deader corpses lay around the nurses' station.

"Is anyone there?" called out Hoskins.

"Lieutenant, is that you?"

"Yes."

"It's Sergeant Murphy. The coast is clear."

Hoskins moved past Ken onto the floor. Murphy and Costas stood outside a hospital room at the end of the corridor, waving. He headed toward them with Alissa and Ken bringing up the rear. It took them a few seconds to negotiate their way around the bodies. When they reached the others, the lieutenant and Murphy fist bumped.

Alissa motioned down the hall. "I see you've been busy."

"Alissa!" Kiera burst out of the room and hugged her.

"You have no idea how glad I am to see you."

Alissa held her tight. "Same here, kid."

"I'm sorry I got mad at you."

A muffled bark came from the room. Shithead raced through the crowd and jumped on Alissa. She removed the gauze from around his mouth, being rewarded with a face bath.

Rebecca joined them. "I'm not going to lick you."

"I can hope."

The two women hugged.

"How's Nathan?"

"No change."

"Is the bus out front?" asked Murphy.

"No," replied Hoskins. "It got stuck a quarter of a mile down the road. We'll have to go to it."

Rogers glanced over to the bed where Nathan lay. "That's a long way to carry someone."

Hoskins agreed. "There's two Humvees out front. We'll use them. Let's get out of here."

Rogers hoisted Nathan on his shoulders in a fireman's carry and Kiera threw a blanket over him. With Hoskins and Ken in the lead, they made their way down the corridor.

When they reached the stairs, Rogers asked, "Can we take the elevator?"

"No problem." Ken pushed the call button.

The doors opened and two deaders lunged out, tackling Ken and shoving him against the nurses' station. One bit his shoulder, the other his upper left arm. Ken clutched the head of the deader ravaging his shoulder and grabbed the other by the belt, holding them in place. He looked over at the others and yelled, "Go."

Hoskins led the group downstairs.

Alissa stepped over to Ken and removed her Sig Sauer. The deaders, sensing new prey, tried to go after her, but Ken held them in place. Alissa raised the weapon and fired one round into each head. The living dead dropped to the floor. She switched her aim to Ken and hesitated.

Ken's eyes met hers, pleading. "Do it."

"Are you sure?"

He nodded.

Alissa fired two rounds into Ken's head, sparing him from being reanimated. She raced downstairs to join the others waiting for her in the lobby.

"Are you okay?" asked Kiera.

"Yes." Alissa responded without emotion. She headed for the lobby doors. "Come on."

Once in the parking lot, the group stopped.

Rogers muttered, "Shit."

The thirty runners that had escaped from the lobby earlier now wandered through the parking lot. Upon seeing the humans emerge from the lobby, they turned toward their food, snarled, and charged.

Chapter Nine

A PAIR OF large, dark images appeared in the nearby intersection and drew closer. For a moment, Alissa wondered what fresh new nightmare this might be until she heard the shifting of gears and the scraping of metal against asphalt. An air horn blared, clearly audible above the roar of the wind.

Two trucks with attached snowplows turned off the street into the hospital parking lot, pulling beside each other and increasing speed. The deaders charged the vehicles. Nearly twenty went down in the first few seconds, their bodies shattered by the plow blades, spewing limbs and heads across the parking lot. The snow around their corpses turned crimson in blood. The Mack slowed and swung right, circling around Alissa's group. The other did a three-point turn at the end of the parking lot and headed back into the fray in a one-sided demolition derby. The thudding of human flesh against steel was sickening but, in this case, music to Alissa's ears.

The Mack stopped beside the group. A burly man with white, close cropped hair climbed out and approached. He broke into an impish grin.

"Looks like we arrived just in time."

"Don't take this the wrong way," said Alissa, "but who are you and where did you come from?"

"I'm Woody." He extended his hand, which Alissa and Hoskins shook. "The other guy in the cab is Ben. We were stuck at the motor pool preparing the rigs to plow when the shit

hit the fan. We were driving around the island looking for survivors when we heard the explosion and followed it here."

"Thank God you did."

"Excuse me, sir." Rogers shifted Nathan on his back. "He's getting heavy."

Hoskins pointed to the closest Humvee. "Put him in the back."

"Is that the infected patient that caused all the hubbub?" asked Woody.

"He's not infected," answered the lieutenant. "He's immune."

Woody cocked an eyebrow. "Then we have to get him out of here."

"That's the plan."

"Are there any other survivors?" asked Woody.

"Two groups that we know of. The first is down the road in a school bus stuck behind a downed tree. My CO and another Guardsman are trapped in a shed down by the ferry."

"Don't forget Chris and Robson," added Alissa.

"That's right. There's a helicopter that flew in the retrieval team and is waiting to extract us. We lost contact after it left the school."

"Crashed?" asked Woody.

"I'm assuming so. The last we heard, they were heading for the airfield up north."

"No problem. We can get you to all of them. Let's do the bus first." Woody headed for the Mack, calling out over his shoulder. "We'll lead the way."

Rogers had put Nathan in the back of the closest Humvee, placing his feet on the deck and resting his head between the rear seats. Rebecca took the seat on the right and Shithead jumped into the one on the left. Kiera rode shotgun. Alissa climbed into the driver's side after first removing a severed hand missing three fingers that had been blown into the cab when the ambulance exploded. The four soldiers took the other

Humvee.

Hoskins beeped the horn three times. Woody blared the airhorn in reply and led the convoy out of the parking lot, each vehicle running over deader corpses and body parts. The vehicles turned right onto Main Street and headed for the bus.

"WE'VE GOT COMPANY," warned Ramircz.

Boyce joined him at the front of the bus. "I hope it's not deaders."

"Not unless the dead have headlights." He pointed ahead of them as a set of bright lights emerged from the storm. A Mack with a plow appeared, engaged in a three-point turn, and backed up to the fallen tree.

"Who are they?" asked Patricia.

"I don't know," said Ramirez. "Thank God they arrived when they did."

Two men climbed out of the first truck and examined the tree. The older of the two motioned to his partner who ran back to the cab and emerged a few seconds later with a chain saw. Hoskins appeared beside the older man. They talked for a minute, then the lieutenant made his way to the bus. Three soldiers spread out around the tree, protecting the workers.

Ramirez opened the door for the lieutenant.

"What's up, sir?" asked Boyce.

"We rescued the group from the hospital and commandeered two Humvees parked out front. They're waiting for us farther down the road."

"Is Alissa okay?" The question came from a worried Susie.

"Alissa is fine, though we lost Ken fighting our way out of the hospital."

Ramirez glanced through the windshield. "Who are they?"

"A local road crew that had been searching the island for survivors. Luckily, they found us when they did or we wouldn't have made it out. Once they're through clearing the road, we're going to rescue Saunders and Ames, see if we can locate our missing helicopter, and then get off this island."

"Not soon enough for me," said Boyce.

Ramirez closed his eyes and muttered a prayer in Spanish.

As those inside the bus watched, Woody and Ben cut the center portion of the tree into small enough sections so the bus could push them aside.

THE SOUND OF the Seahawk flying overhead earlier had disturbed hundreds of deaders from their semi-frozen inactivity, mostly those in Islesboro where almost a thousand deaders stood covered in snow. The explosion of the ambulance, followed by the two trucks driving through town, stirred them into action. Noise meant humans. Humans meant food. Trudging through the drifts, they made their way to the hospital. However, by the time the horde reached the parking lot, all they found were crushed deaders and the smoldering remains of a charred ambulance.

A muffled sound caught their attention – the high-pitched roar of a chainsaw. Noise meant humans. Humans meant food.

As one, the horde followed the sound and shambled south down Main Street.

ALISSA HAD TURNED the Humvee around and parked facing north, leaving the engine idling. She rolled down the window to better see the rearview mirror, barely making out the outlines of the two trucks in the storm. The whining of chainsaws cutting through wood could be distinguished over the wind. With luck, they would be back on the road in a few minutes.

A moaning from the back seat broke through Alissa's thoughts.

"You need to see this," said Rebecca.

Alissa closed her eyes. She had been expecting this moment ever since Nathan had been bitten. Figures it would happen now during this Grade A cluster fuck. Withdrawing her Sig Sauer from its holster, she shifted in her seat and lowered the barrel toward the top of his skull.

"Sit back so you don't get hurt."

"This is how you greet me?" asked Nathan.

"You're awake." Alissa quickly switched the weapon to her left hand and then cupped Nathan's cheek in her right. "I thought I'd lost you."

"New Englanders don't go down easy. You should know that." Nathan huffed several times to catch his breath.

"Relax. You've been through a lot."

"I remember being bit during the attack on the cabin. How long have I been out?"

"Close to three days."

"Not that I'm complaining…." Nathan forced a weak smile. "Why haven't I turned?"

"You fought off the virus. However, you developed an infection from the bacteria left behind when the deader bit you."

"And you've been with me the entire time?"

"Most of it."

Nathan tried to raise a hand to clasp Alissa's but did not have the strength. Instead, he twisted to one side and kissed her palm. When he did, he noticed Rebecca seated beside him. She smiled and offered a half wave. Shithead bent his head and licked Nathan's other cheek.

Kiera leaned forward from the passenger seat. "Glad to see you're feeling better."

Nathan became confused. His eyes roamed around the interior of the Humvee. "Where are we?"

"An island off the coast of Maine," answered Kiera.

"How did we get to Maine?" Nathan tried to sit up.

Alissa gently pushed him back into a prone position. "It's been an unusual three days."

Rebecca chuckled. "That's an understatement."

"Take it easy," said Alissa. "I'll fill you in on all the details once we're out of here."

"Are we safe?"

"For now, yes."

"You might want to rephrase that." Kiera tapped Alissa's arm and pointed through the windshield.

One hundred feet ahead of them, a deader appeared out of the blizzard, following the path cleared moments earlier by the plows. As they watched, more and more shadows emerged from the snow, all of them bearing down on the Humvee.

Chapter Ten

"WE HAVE TO warn the others," said Rebecca.

Alissa searched the dashboard and console. "Fuck."

"What?"

"Hoskins has both radios. We can't contact him."

"What are we going to do?"

Kiera leaned forward and glanced upward through the windshield. "Yes."

"What is it?" asked Alissa.

"This Humvee has a mounted fifty."

"So?"

"Chris taught me how to use one, remember?"

Before Alissa could respond, Kiera crouched on the seat, slid aside the access door, and sat on the thin strap the gunner's normally use. She removed the weather cover, cracked open the ammunition can and fed the link into the tray, worked the charging handle twice, swiveled the weapon toward the targets, and depressed the butterfly triggers in short, controlled burps.

Fifty caliber rounds cut across the road, ripping the first deader in half and blowing apart those behind them.

A STACCATO SOUND cut through the night, audible over the noise generated by the chainsaws. At first Costas ignored it until it repeated a second and third time. Checking his surroundings for any apparent threats, he made his way over to Woody and tapped him on the back.

Woody stopped cutting through the tree. "What?"

"Stop the chainsaws for a minute. I hear something but can't make it out."

Woody shut down his chainsaw and waved to catch Ben's attention. When Ben turned to him, Woody pointed to the chainsaw and waved his hand across his throat. The area went silent, but only for a few seconds. Then the distinct chatter of machine gun fire came from where they had left the other Humvee.

"How much more time do you need?" Costas asked Woody.

"Another minute or two." Woody and Ben went back to cutting.

Costas ran back to the bus to warn Hoskins.

HOSKINS NOTICED THE sergeant racing toward the bus. "This doesn't look good."

Ramirez pulled open the door so the lieutenant could meet him.

"Sir, we have gunfire coming from the Humvee with the civilians. I'm assuming it's deader activity. Woody says it'll take a few minutes to clear the road."

"Damn it." Hoskins quickly worked out a plan. "Take the second plow and go help the civilians. Leave Murphy and Rogers here in case any deaders get past you or move in from the flanks. We'll join you as soon as we can."

"Yes, sir." Costas saluted and ran off to carry out his orders.

Hoskins waved for Boyce to join him. "Stay here. I'm going to check on the progress in clearing the road."

COSTAS CIRCLED AROUND where Woody and Ben sliced up the tree and rushed past their plow. Rogers and Murphy moved in from the flanks to intersect him.

"Sarge," asked Murphy. "What's going on?"

"We heard gunfire." Rogers stamped his feet against the cold. "It sounds like a fifty."

"I'm taking the first plow to check on that. The road crew is almost done clearing the road, so be prepared to move."

"Gotcha, sarge."

The first plow sat fifty feet away at the head of the column. Costas jumped on the running board and knocked on the driver's window.

Inside the cab, Brad nearly pissed himself. He rolled down the window. "Jesus, man. You scared the shit out of me."

"We need to check out that gunfire up ahead. You up for it?"

"Damn straight. It's about time we started plowing something other than snow." Brad shifted into gear. "Hang on. It might get a little bumpy."

Costas reached into the cab and clasped the back of the seat with his right hand as the truck accelerated.

KIERA USED CONTROLLED bursts to cut down the deaders. The strategy worked for the first few minutes. None of the deaders got to within twenty feet of the Humvee. As the horde drew closer, the number of targets became too great for her to keep under control. She leaned back in the hatch and yelled down to Alissa.

"Where are the others?"

"I assume still trying to clear the road."

"They better hurry. I can't—"

The blare of a truck horn caught their attention. Kiera glanced over her shoulder as one of the plows emerged from the snow heading north on the opposite side of the road. It drove past the Humvee and slammed into the horde on the left lane, pushing through one hundred feet of deaders. The thudding of bodies against the metal blade overpowered the roar of the diesel engines. The truck slowed, stopped, and backed up, its tires leaving two long trails of blood in the snow as well as a pile of mangled bodies. When the annoyingly loud and continuous beep of the back-up warning signal engaged, the noise drove the rest of the deaders into a frenzy. Those not crushed quickened their pace to reach the truck. The vehicle stopped and, thankfully, so did the signal. Shifting into gear, the driver surged forward, this time cutting in front of the Humvee and clearing the right lane of the living dead for one hundred feet. The truck backed up again. Riverlets of crimson wound their way down the asphalt.

The truck maneuvered around the Humvee and stopped by the driver's side. Alissa opened the door and stepped out. As she did, a severed arm dropped from the corner of the plow blade and landed on the road. Gary leaned out the passenger window and waved.

Costas came around the front of the truck. "We came to help you out, but it seems like you were doing a good job on your own."

"We appreciate it."

The sergeant motioned toward the road. Another dozen or so deaders had emerged from the blizzard. "Any idea how many more there are?"

Alissa shook her head. "For each one we take down, two more take its place."

Kiera fired a few more short bursts, killing the closest deaders.

"Don't worry," offered Costas. "They're almost done clearing the road."

WOODY SLICED THROUGH another section of the fallen tree and paused to check their progress. He and Ben had segmented it into two-foot-wide sections extending beyond the school bus's plow blade.

"You should be able to get through now."

"Thanks." Hoskins patted Woody on the back.

"Where's our next stop?"

"We have two men at the station down by the ferry. Are you familiar with it?"

"Of course."

"Good. You and the other plow take the lead."

"Roger that."

Hoskins pointed toward the truck. "Do you have a radio in that thing?"

"Yup."

"Have the other truck tell Alissa to fall in behind you."

"Gotcha."

Woody and Ben rushed off to their plow.

Hoskins waved until he caught the attention of Murphy and Rogers then motioned for them to join him.

"We finally on the move?" asked Murphy.

"Yes. I'm going to stay on the bus. I want you to bring up the rear. You'll need this." The lieutenant handed Murphy a radio.

The corporal took it. "Where are we heading now, in case we get separated?"

"We're going to retrieve Saunders and Ames, then look for our missing pilot."

Murphy and Rogers headed for their Humvee as Hoskins made his way back to the bus. Ramirez opened the door, closing it behind the lieutenant.

"You should be able to push your way through. The trucks

will take the lead and clear a path. Alissa will follow them. You'll follow her. We're heading to the dock area."

Ramirez shifted into drive. When the Mack pulled away, he accelerated. The bus rocked from side to side when it hit the segmented tree but easily pushed the sections out of the way.

Hoskins checked in back. Patricia and Susie were fine. Boyce, who sat behind them, gave him a thumbs up. Hoskins removed the radio from the dashboard and pressed the talk button.

"Captain Saunders, do you copy?"

"SIR, I THINK the storm is letting up."

The captain looked out the window. The snow came down less heavily and visibility had increased. Nine deaders stood motionless nearby, their heads and shoulders covered in several inches of snow, the closest over a hundred feet away.

"Let's be grateful for small favors, private."

"Yes, sir."

Hoskins voice came over the radio. "Captain Saunders, do you copy?"

Saunders keyed the talk button. "I'm here."

"Hang tight, sir. We're on our way to get you now."

"How long do you think you'll be?"

"Fifteen minutes at most."

"Hurry up. We're freezing."

"Don't worry. The bus is nice and warm."

"Good. See you soon."

Saunders tried to stand but found it difficult. The wound did not hurt, but only because his legs were numb from the frigid temperature. He would be lucky if he didn't lose the leg.

"Do you need help, sir?"

"I'm fine. Thanks. Help is on the way."

"I heard, sir."

76

About time, thought Saunders.

KIERA CONTINUED TO take down any deaders that got near the Humvee. Alissa smiled. She was having way too much fun.

Gary leaned out of the cab of his truck.

"Which one of you is Alissa?"

"That's me."

"I just got a call from Woody. The bus is free and they'll be here soon. You're to fall in behind me."

"Will do." She turned to Murphy. "Get in the back. We have room."

Murphy circled around the Humvee and opened the rear door. Shithead barked once and wagged his tail, then jumped into the back. Murphy spotted Nathan and paused.

"It's okay," said Nathan. "I won't bite."

Murphy climbed in and shut the door. "Sorry, sir. No offense."

"None taken."

Alissa tugged on Kiera's leg. She lowered herself into the cab.

"What's up?"

"We're moving out."

"Good. I'm almost out of ammo." Kiera closed the door, dropped into her seat, and buckled in.

The Mack pulled up alongside the other truck and stopped, then both vehicles accelerated, side by side. Alissa fell in a few yards to their rear. She glanced in her mirror. The bus followed a few yards behind, with the second Humvee bringing up the rear.

Ahead of them, the plows slammed into the remaining deaders. Crushed bodies and severed limbs flew off to the sides. The spray from the tires mixed with the blood of the living dead covered the windshield. She switched on the wipers. They cleared away the spray, but blood streaked the glass, though not enough to prevent her from seeing.

A deader in a county police uniform stood in the center of the road. The edge of one of the plows tore off its arm and knocked it off balance. Alissa could not swerve in time to avoid it. The grill smashed into the deader. It bounced onto the hood and across the windshield, ripping off the passenger side wiper before it slid across the roof and off the back. Shithead spun around and barked as it fell into the road, being crushed under the wheels of the school bus.

After a quarter of a mile, they passed through the horde and entered a stretch of isolated road heading north.

The deaders that survived the onslaught, numbering approximately two hundred and fifty, stumbled along after the convoy.

CHRIS STAMPED HIS feet and rubbed his gloved hands together to stay warm. Robson leaned against the bulkhead across from him, his right leg raised, massaging it vigorously. After a minute, he switched legs. When finished, he twisted his upper body from one side to the other.

"You need to keep moving or you'll freeze."

Chris slouched against the rear of the pilot's seat and clutched his wounded leg. "My leg hurts too much."

"All the more reason."

Chris laid his head back. "We're not going to make it out of this alive, are we?"

"I won't lie to you." Robson began doing squats. "It doesn't look good, but I think we'll be fine. The others know we were flying back to the airfield. If they can't reach us by radio, they'll come looking for us."

"Where are they?"

"We're in the middle of a blizzard surrounded by deaders

with groups of survivors spread all over the island. Give them time. We leave no one behind."

"I wish I had your optimism." Chris used his hands to massage his leg as Robson had done. "I'm afraid our luck has run out."

"You're right. If you rely only on luck, then you're living on borrowed time. I don't. I rely on skill, survival instincts, and my buddies. It's how I survived three crash landings, one of them aboard the *Iwo Jima*."

Chris grinned. "*Now* you warn me about all the crash landings."

"That's why I call it Miracle Air." Robson reached over and gave Chris a friendly tap on the shoulder. "Hang in there a little longer. We'll get out of this."

THE CONVOY CONTINUED north for two miles through the center of Islesboro until Main Road branched right toward the northern part of the island. Woody veered left onto West Bay Road and followed it for another three miles, circling around the airfield to the western side of the island. Just before Broad Point Reserve, he turned right onto Ferry Road and led the convoy down to Grindel Point, the location of the terminal. Here the snow was a pristine coating of white spread out across the area, the only things disturbing its beauty being the roofs of several buildings and nine deaders standing in the middle of the parking lot.

Woody continued straight with the other vehicles in tow. Brad broke off into the parking lot, crushing three deaders on his first pass. He made three more sweeps through the lot before eliminating all of them.

Ames ran outside, waving his hands to catch their attention. The convoy stopped with the bus nearest the building. Murphy and Rogers piled out of the last Humvee, the latter guarding the rear of the convoy and the former making his way to the front. Kiera manned the hatch-mounted machine gun and guarded their left flank. Alissa and Woody left their vehicles to join those at the bus, with Costas watching the right flank.

Saunders limped out and made his way through the deep snow. He stumbled after a few feet and fell face down into a drift. Ames and Hoskins rushed over to help. Boyce jumped off the bus and joined them.

"Is he alright?" asked the medic.

"I'm fine," snapped Saunders as the others lifted him to his feet. "It's just a leg wound. Almost freezing to death didn't help."

"Sorry, sir," apologized Hoskins.

"It's not your fault."

Boyce gave the leg a cursory look. "Get him on board."

Hoskins and Ames helped Saunders on the bus and placed him in the front seat opposite Susie and Patricia. He grimaced as he sat, then glanced toward the back.

"Is this everyone?"

"Yes, sir. The rest are in the Humvee, including the patient. We lost Sergeant MacIntyre and one civilian who came back to help."

"Dammit."

Boyce knelt in front of Saunders. "Let me have a look at that leg."

"I thought you left with the others."

"I did. The survivors are waiting for us at Belfast Airport."

"How did you get here?"

"A Navy helicopter flew us back," said Alissa. "We haven't heard from him in hours. We still need to find him and Chris."

"Who's Chris?"

"The civilian who went back to Mass General to obtain the blood samples," explained Hoskins.

"How did that go?"

"They retrieved the blood samples, but all the military

members on that team were killed."

"We're having a fucking cheery day, aren't we?"

Boyce used a pair of scissors to cut open the pants leg. "How bad does it hurt, sir?"

"I can barely feel my leg."

"You have a severe case of frostbite."

"Am I going to lose it?"

"It depends on whether we can get you appropriate medical care."

"Then I guess I'm screwed." Saunders turned to Hoskins. "What now?"

"You're in charge, sir."

Saunders shook his head. "You've done an excellent job so far. I assume you've worked out an exit plan."

"We have. We still need to find our missing people, then we'll grab a boat and join the others back in Belfast. Which reminds me." The lieutenant turned to Ames. "Take Murphy and Rogers and see if there are any boats around we can commandeer."

"Don't bother." Saunders twisted in his seat and placed his leg on the empty one beside him. "We did that during the evacuation. We found only one usable boat, and the others took that to escape."

Alissa sighed. "Then we're stuck here until help arrives, whenever that is."

"Not necessarily." Ramirez joined them. "There's a marina on the southern part of the island. A small tugboat is docked there. We use it to break up ice around the ferry route in the winter. It's probably still there. We could get away in that."

Hoskins turned to his CO. "What do you think, sir?"

"This is your show now." Saunders pointed to his leg. "I'm out of action."

"Okay. Let's find our missing people."

"That might be a problem," said Ramirez. "Assuming they didn't crash, there are a lot places they could have set down, mostly open fields not accessible by road."

Alissa grew concerned. "Robson said he was heading for the airfield. How far is that from here?"

"We passed it. We can check it out on the way back."

"It's settled," said Hoskins. "We go to the airfield, hopefully retrieve our missing people, then head for the marina."

Woody nodded. "I know where the entrance is."

"Let's move, people. I want to be off this island by noon."

Alissa and Woody returned to their vehicles. Costas rounded up Murphy and Rogers and joined them in the last Humvee.

As Alissa climbed into her vehicle, Kiera lowered herself into the troop compartment and closed the hatch.

"Did we get who we needed to?" asked Rebecca.

"Yes, but the CO's leg is in bad shape. He may lose it."

"That sucks." Kiera grimaced. "What now?"

"We think we have a way off the island. First, we're going to find Robson and Chris."

"Do we have to?" asked Nathan.

Alissa shifted in her seat and glared at him.

Nathan leaned his head back and winked. "I'm kidding. Stop being so serious."

After clearing the parking lot of the living dead, Brad pulled his truck alongside of Woody. Both trucks made a U-turn and led the convoy back the way they had come.

FIVE MINUTES LATER, Woody turned right off West Bay Road onto an access road surrounded by trees. A few seconds later, they entered the parking lot of the island's airport.

Ben pointed to the snow-covered remains of the crashed helicopter lying in its side. "I think we found them."

"Let's hope they're still alive." Woody gave a long blare on the air horn.

CHRIS LIFTED HIS head. "Did you hear that?"

"I did." Robson crouched down and peered through the helicopter's shattered windscreen. Two trucks plowed their way toward them. "Someone is coming to save us. I told you not to give up hope."

Chris closed his eyes and prayed Alissa was one of them.

WHEN THE PLOWS veered right, Alissa saw the crashed helicopter. Her heart raced. They had found them. Now she hoped Chris would be alive.

She pulled the Humvee alongside the Seahawk, shifted into park, and jumped out. Running over, she dropped into the snow and stared through the shattered glass.

"Chris, are you there?"

Chris pushed himself off the back of the seat and stood in the opening. "Alissa, is that you?"

"Yes. I'm glad to see you're alive."

Robson leaned over so he could be seen. "I'm alive, too, thank you very much."

A feeling of embarrassment filled Alissa, which turned into shame when she saw the body of Frank hanging from the co-pilot's seat.

Woody joined Alissa and examined the cockpit. "There's too much damage for you to get out this way. Can you climb through the door?"

Robson pointed to Chris. "He'll never make it. His leg is wounded. And to be honest, my legs and hands are too cold to do any climbing."

"Hang tight. We'll have you out of there in a few minutes." Woody headed back to the Mack.

Alissa leaned closer. "Are either of you hurt?"

"Just my leg," answered Chris.

"And freezing our asses off," added Robson.

"Don't worry. The school bus is warm. Be right back."

Robson grinned. "We're not going anywhere."

Alissa joined the others. Hoskins had deployed his troops, including himself, to guard each flank of the work area. Woody climbed into the Mack and backed it up so its rear was perpendicular to the helicopter. Ben removed a chain twenty feet in length with hooks on both ends. He attached one end of the chain to the ball mount on the rear chassis of the Mack and wrapped the other around the port landing gear of the helicopter, securing it in place with the hook. He banged on the underside of the helicopter.

"We're going to pull this thing over so it's sitting upright. I'd hang on to something."

"Roger that," called out Robson.

Ben moved out of the way and circled around to the front of the Mack, signaling Woody. Woody inched the truck forward. The chain grew taut. Ben waved him to continue. The Seahawk teetered. Inside, Chris and Robson held on tightly to the seats. A moment later, the helicopter fell over, landing heavily on its landing gear.

"That was almost as good as my landing," joked Robson.

Chris grunted due to the throbbing in his leg.

As Ben unhooked the chain, Alissa ran over and jumped inside, dropping to her knees and hugging Chris.

"I worried when we didn't hear from you."

Chris embraced her, holding her for several seconds. "A gust of wind tipped us over as we landed. We probably wouldn't be alive if Robson hadn't been such a good pilot."

"Now you're nice to me." Robson stepped up to Chris and offered his hand. "Come on. Let's get out of here and into some place warm."

Alissa and Robson helped him across the deck to the door. Boyce waited outside where he assisted Chris in climbing out. Boyce and Robson each wrapped an arm around their shoulders and escorted Chris to the bus. Alissa stayed close.

Once on the bus, Boyce lowered Chris into the seat behind

Patricia and Susie and gestured for Robson to take the seat opposite. He quickly checked both men.

"Are we going to lose fingers and toes?" asked Robson.

"I don't think so. You both have mild hypothermia but being on the bus will help."

Chris patted his leg. "What about the wound?"

"I don't want to remove the bandage until we're back at a medical facility. It'll be safer that way."

"Without the chopper, how are we going to get there? It'll be a few days before the *Iwo Jima* can send anyone to help."

"We have that covered," said Alissa. "There's a marina down south with a tug. We're going to use it to get to the mainland."

"I hope someone knows how to operate it," said Robson.

Shit. Alissa had not thought of that before.

Chris held Alissa's hand. "What about Nathan and the others?"

"We rescued them all. Kiera and Rebecca are fine. And Nathan is conscious."

"What about Shithead?"

"He's fine. He'll turn himself inside out when he sees you."

"Good."

Woody boarded the bus. "We're all set."

"You know how to get there?" Alissa asked.

"We both do," answered Ramirez.

"One second." Alissa held Chris' cheeks in her hands and kissed him. "See you aboard the tug."

She stepped off the bus and made her way back to her Humvee, climbing into the driver's seat.

"How's Chris?" Kiera asked with a little too much concern.

"Chris and the pilot are both well. Unfortunately, the co-pilot died in the crash."

Rebecca mumbled a silent prayer.

Ahead of them, Woody and Brad circled the trucks around the remains of the helicopter and drove back to the exit. The rest of the convoy fell in behind. Once back on West Bay Road, they turned right and proceeded south.

THE SURVIVING DEADERS that the convoy had plowed through at Islesboro had set off after the retreating vehicles, the desperate need for food driving the useless chase. The same instinct that drove them relentlessly after the prey would have kept them on Main Road and diverted them to the northern part of Warren Island. However, two and a half feet of snow blocked the road. The branch that bore left – West Bay Road – had been cleared earlier by the convoy and offered the path of least assistance. The horde staggered in that direction.

Directly into the path of the approaching convoy.

Chapter Eleven

B OTH TRUCKS ROUNDED the bend into a horde of over two hundred deaders. Woody pressed his foot on the gas pedal. The Mack lurched forward, clearing fifty to sixty of the living dead. Caught by surprise, Brad swerved to the right to avoid hitting them. His truck slammed into the accumulated snow along the side of the road and dropped down the embankment. The rest of the convoy stopped, with Alissa's Humvee being closest to the stuck vehicle.

The surviving deaders converged on them.

Woody grabbed the microphone from the dashboard and keyed the talk button.

"Brad, are you okay?"

No answer.

"Can you hear me, Brad?"

Still no answer.

Woody opened the driver's door and started to get out when Ben grabbed his arm.

"You need to drive this thing or none of us are getting out of here. I'll check on them."

Ben threw open his door and started to climb out. A deader in its underwear stumbled toward him. Ben kicked it in the face, breaking its jaw. It staggered back a few feet. Ben jumped to the road, slipping on the compacted snow and falling onto his knees. Before he could stand, the underwear deader lunged, knocking him over and pinning him to the ground.

FROM ALISSA'S POSITION, she could see deaders bearing down on them from the left. They did not have much time. She opened the door, grabbed her carbine, and jumped out, then leaned back into the cab.

"Kiera—"

"I got this." Kiera had slid open the hatch and manned the machine gun.

Alissa circled around behind the Mack. Ben lay in the snow to her left, a deader clawing at him. Three more closed in. She changed direction and went to help.

HOSKINS CURSED THEIR luck when he saw the plow on the right swerve and go off the road. Then he noticed the deaders descending on the crash site. He grabbed his carbine with one hand and the radio with the other.

"Costas, we need firepower up here."

Before waiting for a reply, the lieutenant opened the sliding door to the bus and jumped onto the road.

"COSTAS, WE NEED firepower up here."

Costas, Murphy, and Rogers exited their Humvee at the rear of the line and rushed in to join the fray.

THE UNDERWEAR DEADER had its upper jaw pressed against Ben's arm but could not bite through because of the shattered lower half. Alissa raced up and kicked it in the face, knocking it backward. Raising her carbine, she fired a single round into its head, then did the same for the three closest deaders. Ben had begun to crawl to his feet. Alissa wrapped her free hand around his arm and helped him to the truck.

"Thanks."

"Don't mention it. Save your friends so we can get out of

here."

As Alissa took up guard position by the front fender, Ben jumped onto the running board and peered inside.

"Brad, are you okay?"

"Yes." Brad leaned over the passenger seat, unbuckling the belt. "Gary hit his head and is unconscious. Help me get him out."

Ben jumped down, rushed around to the other side, and opened the door. Brad had unbuckled Gary and held him upright by the collar so the man didn't fall out. He moved over into the passenger seat and grabbed Gary by his underarms.

"Take his legs and pull him out."

WOODY WATCHED THE rescue from behind his steering wheel when he heard a snarl to his left. A deader he recognized as his next-door neighbor closed in on him. Woody kicked the door all the way open, smashing the outer surface against its face. Shutting it so nothing could get to him, he shifted into gear and drove forward three hundred feet. Several of the deaders followed, clasping at the side of the truck to get at the food inside.

WHEN THE MACK pulled away, it allowed Kiera a clear field of fire. She released controlled bursts, taking out any deaders that neared the snow-bound truck or the Humvee. More than a hundred still bore down on them in the right lane. She knew she did not have enough ammunition to eliminate them all.

HOSKINS REACHED THE truck as Brad and Ben removed Gary from the cab. The others joined him a few seconds later.

"Is he alive?" asked the lieutenant.

"Just knocked himself out in the accident," responded Brad.

"Get him on the bus."

KIERA AIMED AT a bloated deader in a grey sweatshirt and Red Sox baseball cap, the former pushed up to its chest by the extended stomach. A round struck its abdomen, tearing off the upper torso. Undigested human flesh spewed from the ruptured stomach onto the blood-stained snow, sending the stench of bodily fluids and gases wafting over the road. The last three rounds caught the deader in its head, shattering it. The body collapsed.

The belt to the machine gun no longer showed.

"Is there another case of ammo down there?"

Rebecca searched the twin seat wells in back as well as the rear deck. "Nothing."

"Shit." Kiera banged on the Humvee's roof to attract Alissa's attention. "I'm out of ammo. Get back to the Humvee."

"I'm covering the others."

"They're heading to the school bus."

Without the fire from the machine gun, a dozen deaders had drawn closer to the convoy, cutting Alissa off from the Humvee.

Kiera ducked back into the cab and started to open the door when Rebecca leaned forward and grabbed her collar.

"Let me go. I have to save Alissa."

"You'll only get yourself killed."

CHRIS HAD BEEN watching the battle play out from his seat on the bus, frustrated that he could not help. When he saw Alissa being surrounded by deaders, he jumped out of his seat to rescue her.

Boyce blocked his path. "Sit down."

"I have to help Alissa."

"You won't make it twenty feet on that leg and then we'll

have to save your sorry ass as well. Sit."

Chris obeyed, reluctantly.

Boyce exited the bus and ran over to help with Gary. "Alissa is in trouble."

Hoskins turned and saw the approaching pack. "Rogers, Murphy. Help her out."

As the two soldiers raced down the road, the rest carried Gary aboard the bus.

A DOZEN DEADERS gathered around the front of Woody's truck, scratching at the doors to get inside. He did not worry about them. Instead, he watched in his side mirror events play out at the crash site, breathing a sigh of relief when he saw the others had saved Brad and Gary. Relief turned to frustration when he noticed a dozen deaders had trapped Alissa around the stranded vehicle.

Woody shifted into reverse. The beeping of the back-up signal drove the deaders around the Mack into a frenzy. He maneuvered into the right lane and accelerated. Ten of the deaders shifted their attention from Alissa to the truck and went after the new prey. Woody slammed into them with the rear of the Mack, knocking them under the wheels where the weight of the truck exploded them like ketchup packets, splattering blood and guts across the snow. He stopped the truck twenty feet from Alissa.

She took the opportunity and ran, easily dodging the last two deaders.

As she reached the Humvee, Rogers and Murphy arrived, taking down the pair with headshots.

Alissa paused. "Thanks."

Murphy waved and he and Rogers fell back to their vehicle.

Woody leaned out the Mack's window. "Are you okay?"

"I'm fine," yelled Alissa. "Head to the marina. We'll follow."

Woody shifted into drive and proceeded down Main Road, crashing into the pack of deaders blocking his path.

Alissa jumped in the Humvee and followed, with the rest of the convoy behind her.

Only a handful of the living dead remained, each reaching out for the vehicles as they passed. Within a few seconds, the convoy cleared the danger zone and headed for the marina.

THE REST OF the trip went by without incident. They continued to the hospital where Main Road became Pendleton Pond Road and continued to the location of the fallen tree. A minute later, the convoy passed the access road to the school. A handful of deaders wandered around where they had followed the bus after the initial encounter. The Mack tore right through them.

Less than a mile later, Woody turned right onto the access road to the marina, which led past the office and repair facilities. Circling to the right, the convoy wound its way between the storage buildings and rows of stacked boats before entering the parking area in front of the dock. Woody pulled off to the right and parked by a stack of small boats. Alissa drove the Humvee up to the end of the dock, bouncing over something hidden under the snow. The other two vehicles parked behind her. The dock extended one hundred feet into the ice-encrusted water, with the tug tied to the far end.

"We made it." Kiera leaned to the side and offered her right fist to Alissa.

"I won't be satisfied until we're off this island." Alissa bumped the fist, then shifted to look at Nathan. "I'll be back for you in a minute."

"Take your time. It's comfortable here on this hard deck."

Alissa ruffled his hair and climbed out along with Kiera, the latter leaving her door open. Shithead took advantage of the opportunity. He barked, jumped over the seat, and ran after Alissa.

Chris hobbled off the bus and, on seeing his dog, called to him. Shithead's tail wagged furiously. He barked twice and raced through the snow toward his master, jumping into his arms and giving Chris a face bath. Alissa and Kiera joined them.

Alissa smiled. "Somebody missed you."

"I thought you missed me, too."

"I did, but not enough to lick your face."

"I will," said Kiera flirtatiously.

Alissa and Chris turned to her and simultaneously replied, "No."

Kiera shrugged. "I tried."

Ames helped Saunders off the bus while Costas did the same for Patricia and Susie. Hoskins, Ramirez, and Ben exited last.

Woody walked up to the group. "What now?"

Hoskins gestured toward the dock. "We get aboard the tug and get out of here. Do you know how to operate it?"

Woody shook his head. "Can't stand boats. They scare the shit out of me."

"Does anyone here know how to operate one?"

Patricia stepped forward. "My husband owned a speed boat that I knew how to use, if that'll be of any help."

"It's good enough for me." Hoskins noticed Murphy and Roger approaching. "You two, escort Patricia and the young lady to the tug and make sure it's clear. Patricia knows how to operate it."

"Roger that, sir."

BRAD KNELT ON the seat in front of where Gary lay, watching Boyce check his vital signs. "Will he be all right, doc?"

"He should be, though the chances are good he'll have a

concussion. Your friend will be fine once we get him to a hospital."

"Do you have a stretcher we can put him on?"

Boyce shook his head. "I can fireman's carry him."

"WHAT'S GOING ON?" asked Nathan. "Why is it taking so long?"

"I don't know." Rebecca sat sideways and looked out the rear window at the group gathered around the bus. "Looks like they're planning something."

"As long as it's our escape."

MURPHY AND ROGERS led the way across the parking area to the head of the dock, scanning their front and flanks.

"I'm cold," whined Susie as she pushed her way through the accumulated snow.

"I know. Just keep going. We'll be aboard the tug in a few minutes."

"But my feet are wet and I can't feel—" Susie tripped and fell face first, disappearing in the drift.

Patricia bent over and pulled her up, brushing the snow off her face. "Are you okay?"

"Yes." Susie began to cry. "I tripped over something."

Patricia glanced into the snow to see what caused Susie to stumble. Her eyes widened in terror.

"Dear fucking God."

SHITHEAD STOPPED LICKING Chris and growled. His ears folded back and his tail curled between his legs. For a moment, Alissa thought the dog might attack Chris. Shithead dropped off his master and stared out into the parking lot, the growling becoming more intense. Hoskins raised his carbine, took several steps away from the bus, and scanned the area in a three-hundred-sixty-degree arc. Nothing approached from behind the buildings or stacks of boats.

"Does anyone see deaders?" he yelled.

The others were also looking for danger but could not see anything.

A hand shot out of the snow and clutched Alissa by the knee. She cried out. A second hand reached out and grabbed her leg. A deader pulled itself up, hand by hand, dragging itself onto Alissa.

All around the marina, close to thirty deaders stood from where they had been covered in snow.

Chapter Twelve

THE WEIGHT OF the deader climbing up Alissa knocked her off balance. She fell against the bus.

Shithead reacted first. He leapt from in front of Chris to Alissa, ripping the deader off her and pinning it to the ground. Hoskins rushed over, pushed the dog out of the way, and fired a round into the deader's skull.

Another thirteen of the living dead surrounded the bus and surged in for the kill.

ROGERS RUSHED OVER to Patricia and Susie, inserting himself between the women and the deader buried in the snow. He ushered them to one side. The deader opened its eyes and snarled. Rogers put two rounds into its head.

Murphy raised his carbine and turned to Patricia. "You ladies, on my six."

Murphy headed down the dock with Patricia and Susie huddled close behind him. Rogers brought up the rear.

"WHAT THE FUCK?" Rebecca shifted in her seat to gaze out the rear window.

"Is everything okay?" asked Nathan. He could tell by the terrified expression on her face it wasn't.

"Deaders are buried all over the parking lot."

"We have to help them." Nathan futilely tried to sit up.

Rebecca placed a hand on his shoulder and pushed him down. "You're in no shape to—"

Something thudded against the window beside Rebecca. She cried out. A deader in a National Guard uniform, the skin and tissue chewed off its right arm, clutched at the window with its left hand. Its teeth scraped against the glass. Rebecca futilely searched the cab for a weapon.

Thwarted in its efforts, the deader stumbled around the Humvee, searching for a way to get in. As it moved around to the passenger side, Rebecca realized Kiera had left her door open. Jumping up, she crawled between the front seats, desperate to close it. She slipped and fell, picked herself up, and reached for the handle.

The deader centered itself in the door and snarled.

BOYCE NOTICED THE dead rising out of the snow. They had minutes at most to get Gary to safety.

"Can you carry your friend by yourself?"

"Yes," Brad replied.

"Good." Boyce grabbed his carbine and moved to the front of the bus. "Let's go."

Brad lifted Gary in a fireman's carry and joined the medic.

A DEADER ROUNDED the rear of the bus and shambled toward those gathered by the door. Hoskins took it down with a single shot to the head.

Another deader crawled underneath the vehicle. It grabbed Ramirez by the ankles and yanked, dropping him face first into the snow and dragging him under the vehicle. Ramirez rolled over and grabbed the chassis, holding on for dear life and kicking at its face to break free.

"Get me out of here," he screamed.

Hoskins and Costas each grabbed an arm and pulled, but

the deader refused to let go. It crawled farther up Ramirez until it reached his upper leg. Panic overcame him, which turned into resignation when he felt its teeth dig into his flesh.

"Fuck!"

Ames leaned Saunders against the side of the bus, fell prone, and fired into the deader's head. Without the weight holding Ramirez down, Hoskins and Costas were able to pull him free.

The lieutenant stared at the fatal wound. "I'm sorry, man."

Ramirez leaned against the bus, wincing from the pain. "Give me your pistol."

"I'll do it for you if you want."

Ramirez shook his head. "I'm going to distract these mother fuckers as long as possible."

Hoskins unholstered his Sig Sauer and handed it to him. "Good luck and God bless."

"Thanks."

The lieutenant turned to the others. "Let's move or we're dead."

Alissa heard a scream coming from the Humvee. A deader climbed inside to get at Nathan and Rebecca. She bolted from the others to go help them.

Kiera ran after her, pausing long enough to call Shithead. The dog looked up at Chris for guidance.

"Go help Alissa."

Shithead bounded through the snow.

HAVING NO WEAPON, Woody ran over to his Mack, body-checking out of the way a deader in civilian clothes. Once at the truck, he removed an ice breaker from its mount on the side of the vehicle and raced back.

The deader he had shoved aside started to rise back to its feet. Woody swung the ice breaker like a baseball bat, smashing the weapon into the side of its head. The deader collapsed face first. Woody raised the blade and brought it down on the deader's neck, severing its spine. It lurched and moaned in protest. He continued chopping at the neck until its head tore free from its body and the deader went limp.

BOYCE EXITED THE bus to join the others. Three deaders stood between them and the dock.

Hoskins fired a round into the head of the closest, dropping it. He did the same to the second. The bolt on his carbine locked back.

"I'm out."

As the lieutenant reloaded, Boyce stepped forward and fired two rounds into the third deader. One punched into its chest with no effect. The last tore its head from its body.

"Move."

Hoskins and Costas led the way. Ames followed, helping Saunders. Robson assisted Chris. Brad and Ben fell in behind them, the former carrying Gary. Boyce brought up the rear.

MURPHY REACHED THE tug and helped Patricia and Susie on board.

Rogers jumped on. "What now?"

"Can you start this thing?" asked Murphy.

Patricia nodded. "I think so."

"Then let's get to pilothouse."

Rogers led the way to the bow.

RAMIREZ BANGED HIS left hand against the side of the bus and yelled to attract the deaders' attention.

"Come on, you fucking sacks of meat. Get your nice, warm meal and give me a chance to send you all to Hell."

The seven closest to the bus moved in for the kill while the rest pursued the others.

Ramirez aimed at the nearest deader, its eyes frozen shut, and fired a single round that hit the center of its forehead. It staggered a moment then continued its advance. He fired again, this time lower, ripping off its lower jaw and dropping the body. Switching to another, Ramirez took it down with three shots, then continued the attack and killed two more until the slide on the Sig Sauer locked in the open position. He had hoped to take his own life with the last bullet and be spared the fate of the living dead, but had lost that opportunity when he misjudged the number of rounds he had remaining. His options were limited.

Ramirez yelled at the top of his lungs and charged the remaining three deaders. He bodychecked the nearest, knocking it over. Dropping to his knees and using the Sig Sauer as a hammer, he bashed its skull repeatedly until the bones shattered and caved in. Even then, he continued pummeling its head until he destroyed the limbic system and it stopped moving.

The second deader moved up behind him, bent forward, and sunk its teeth into the back of Ramirez' neck. Ramirez groaned from the pain. Reaching behind him over his shoulder, he felt the thing's face. Upon finding its eyes, he jammed his index and middle fingers through the orbs until his knuckles struck the sockets. The deader continued to feed.

The third staggered in front of Ramirez and fell on him, pushing him back into the snow. One of his kneecaps ruptured from the weight. The deader landed on him, its mouth falling on the front of Ramirez' neck. Ramirez attempted to punch it in the side of the head but had grown too weak. The deader bit deep and arched its head back, tearing out a portion of his larynx. Ramirez choked on his own blood, coughing and hacking until he died.

REBECCA FELL BACK into her seat as the deader climbed inside. It crawled between the two seats. She kicked it several times with her boot. The third strike dislocated its bottom jaw. The thing persisted in reaching for its prey.

Shithead reached the Humvee first. He grabbed it by its leg and pulled. The deader lost its footing and fell onto the console. Shithead continued yanking on its leg, preventing it from getting to his friends.

Alissa arrived next. Grabbing the other leg, she yanked the deader out of the Humvee. Using the butt of her carbine, she bashed it repeatedly in the head until its skull caved in.

Making her way to the rear of the vehicle, she opened the hatch and tapped Nathan on the leg.

"It's about time you showed up."

Alissa smiled. "I'm getting tired of saving your ass."

Rebecca jumped out and moved to the back. The two women lifted Nathan, wrapping an arm around each of their shoulders. Alissa handed Kiera the carbine and pouch of spare ammunition.

"Cover us."

"With pleasure."

The group made their way to the dock.

HOSKINS LED THE others toward the dock. As they passed the Mack, a hand reached up out of the snow and grabbed Brad by the leg. He tripped and dropped Gary. The deader flipped over and attacked Gary, sinking its teeth into the unconscious man's neck.

Brad jumped up and grabbed the deader by the hair, pulling it off Gary. The thing's scalp came off in his hands. It spun around and lunged at Brad, biting him in the thigh and tearing out a chunk of flesh. Blood spurted from the severed artery, shooting out onto the snow where it steamed.

Costas rammed the stock of his carbine against the side of

the deader's head, knocking it down. Hoskins stepped up and fired a single round into its head.

Boyce fell to his knees and checked the two wounded men. He glanced up at the lieutenant and shook his head.

Woody joined them. "How bad are they hurt?"

"They've both been bitten," Boyce answered.

Brad knelt in the snow, his eyes pleading. "Don't let me die like this."

Hoskins raised his carbine but Woody placed his hand on the barrel and lowered it. "Let me do it."

"Are you sure?"

Woody nodded.

Hoskins motioned for Costas to give Woody his Sig Sauer, which he did.

Woody aimed the weapon at Brad's head. "Sorry, buddy."

"Don't be." Brad forced a smile. "Thank you."

Woody fired a single round that entered Brad's forehead. When he hit the snow, Woody fired one more round into his head and two into Gary's, then handed the weapon to Hoskins.

"Keep it. You'll need it."

Nine deaders shambled toward them, none close enough to pose an immediate danger.

"Let's get to the boat."

ROGERS CLIMBED THE outer stairs of the tug and paused at the landing to the pilothouse. He tried the door. It was unlocked.

He turned to Murphy. "Things are finally breaking—"

The captain of the tug, dead for two days, lunged from inside the pilothouse. Being freshly reanimated and not effected by the cold, it possessed full mobility. It struck the door hard, flinging it open, and landed on Rogers. Both tumbled over the gunwale and onto the ice surrounding the vessel, breaking through into the freezing water beneath. Rogers let go of his carbine and elbowed the deader in the face, breaking its grip.

The deader sank beneath the surface. Rogers knew what would happen if he became trapped under the ice and desperately swam for the hole he had fallen through.

He broke through and called out to Murphy. "Throw me a line."

The corporal searched around for something. Patricia handed him a life ring with a rope attached. "Use this."

Murphy held the loose end of the rope and tossed the ring over the side. It landed in the water two feet from Rogers. The private swam over to it.

The sinking deader reached out and clasped Rogers' ankle, pulling him under. He attempted to kick free but the deader held on, its weight dragging them both deeper into the bay. The ring floated three feet above him. Rogers strained not to breathe, his only hope being to free himself and head for the surface. Running his free foot along his ankle, he broke the deader's fingers. It released him and dropped to the bottom. Rogers swam for the surface. His lungs strained, desperate for air. Just a few more—

Unable to hold out any longer, Rogers inhaled. Ice cold water poured down his windpipe and into his lungs. The shock froze him. His hand broke the surface, scraping against the ring. Then his body sank. His last vision before he died was of Murphy on the pilothouse landing, leaning over the side and reaching for him.

SUSIE HUGGED PATRICIA, crying against her chest. The woman stroked the girl's hair and reassured her everything would be okay.

Murphy turned to them. "Wait here."

"You're not leaving us?"

"I need to make sure the pilothouse is clear. I'll be right back."

Raising his carbine, Murphy entered the pilothouse, scanning all four corners before moving to the center. An open door on the rear wall led below deck. He approached it, stopping five feet away.

"Is anyone down there?"

Silence.

Murphy raced forward, closed and locked the door, then headed back to the landing. He waved the women inside.

"It's all yours."

Patricia released Susie. "You stay right by me."

"I will."

Patricia studied the console for a moment, then selected and pressed a green button.

A roar sounded from the engine room and the vessel vibrated. She glanced at Murphy and grinned.

"Impressive," said the corporal.

"Thanks."

"I assume you can operate it?"

"Good enough to get us to the mainland."

"Excellent." Murphy headed for the door. "Both of you stay here."

"Where are you going?" Patricia asked nervously.

"I'm checking on the others."

Murphy stepped out on the landing and scanned the dock, hoping the others had made it safely.

ALISSA AND REBECCA half carried and half dragged Nathan while Kiera watched for deaders. They reached the tug and paused, wondering how to get Nathan over the gunwale.

"I can board on my own," he said.

"You can't even stand."

"Sure, I can." Nathan pushed the two women away and immediately collapsed. They caught him.

"Asshole," said Alissa under her breath.

Ben broke from his group and ran forward. "I can take

him."

"Are you sure?"

Ben nodded. He threw Nathan over his shoulder in a fireman's carry and cautiously boarded the tug, careful not to slip.

From the landing, Murphy called, "Bring him up here."

Alissa motioned to Rebecca. "Go with them and keep an eye on Nathan. I'll join you in a few."

Ben and Rebecca headed for the pilothouse. Alissa and Kiera waited for the others, assisting Ames and Robson with getting Saunders and Chris on board. Boyce and Costas jumped on, taking firing position along the starboard gunwale. Hoskins and Woody were the last to board. The closest deader was still twenty yards away and moving slowly.

Alissa looked up at the landing and yelled. "Everyone is on board."

She did not notice the deader buried under the snow rising on the aft deck.

MURPHY GLANCED OVER his shoulder to Patricia. "They're all on board."

"Tell them to cast off."

Murphy relayed the order. Woody moved forward to detach the bow moor line from the deck fitting. Hoskins stepped over to Alissa, who blocked the aft fitting.

"Excuse me, ma'am."

Alissa moved to the right, directly in front of the deader rising out of the snow.

Both men signaled Murphy that the lines were free, who passed the information on to Patricia. She steered the wheel to port and revved the engines more than intended. The tug pulled away from the dock and lurched forward, knocking off balance everyone on deck. Saunders dropped out of Ames' arms, landing onto the metal stairs on his wounded leg and crying out. Costas fell forward, grabbing the gunwale before he toppled over the side. Kiera slipped and fell back against the bulkhead, spotting the deader approaching Alissa.

"Alissa, behind you."

Alissa spun around. The lurching of the boat threw her and the snow-encrusted deader off balance. It fell forward, its forehead striking Alissa's left eye. The two tumbled onto the deck, the deader landing on top of Alissa. For a second, her vision blurred. She placed her hand on its chest and ran it up until it struck the chin, then locked her elbow. The deader snarled and snapped at her fingers. Kiera raced over and drove the stock of her carbine into its forehead, sprawling it on the deck. Hoskins grabbed Alissa and pulled her to safety. Once clear, Kiera fired two rounds into the deader's head.

Hoskins helped Alissa to her feet. "Were you bit?"

"I don't know." Alissa held her breath as she examined her hands and, finding no bites there, ran the palms across her face. She exhaled heavily when she saw no blood. "I'm good."

As Kiera hugged her, the lieutenant motioned to Boyce and Costas. "Throw that damn thing overboard."

"Yes, sir." The two picked up the corpse and tossed it into the bay where it sank beneath the surface.

With the deck clear and the tug underway, they made their way to the pilothouse.

Chapter Thirteen

PATRICIA NAVIGATED THE tug south through the channel between Warren Island to the east and the state park to the west, cruising toward West Penobscot Bay. Hoskins and Costas stayed with her, each keeping watch to port and starboard. After searching the crew compartment, Ames and Murphy checked out the engine room. With no deaders lurking below, the rest of the group went down to relax. The crew compartment was not spacious, modern, or luxurious, but it was warm and indoors. It consisted primarily of a table on the port side running the length of the cabin with an L-shaped bench around it. Two sets of bunk beds sat opposite it against the starboard bulkhead.

Saunders reclined on the first bunk as Boyce tended to his wound with the tug's first aid kit. Chris and Nathan rested on the next one in line, seated on the mattress with their backs to the bulkhead. Robson slept in the top bunk. Ben stood at the counter making a pot of coffee. Woody sat by himself at one end of the bench, his elbows resting on the table, his eyes staring off into space, obviously coming to grips with having to take his friend's life. The women sat at the other end of the bench, Rebecca keeping an eye on Susie and Kiera entertaining the young girl. Shithead had curled up beside Kiera and napped. Alissa felt so proud of Kiera. Despite everything she had been through in the past twenty-four hours, she focused her attention on Susie, playing and joking with her, helping the young girl deal with the trauma of losing her family, watching her world crumble around her, and nearly being killed herself. Alissa wished she had Kiera's resilience.

Chris called out to her in a hushed voice. When Alissa met his gaze, he slid over on the mattress and tapped the spot between him and Nathan. She joined them.

"How do you both feel?"

"Like I've had the flu," said Nathan.

"What are your symptoms?"

"I'm exhausted and barely have the energy to move. My muscles ache. And I have a horrible craving."

Alissa involuntarily moved closer to Chris. "For what?"

Nathan focused his eyes on Alissa. "Pancakes."

Alissa and Chris stared at each other for a moment and laughed, one of those boisterous laughs that made everyone in the cabin stare at them.

"What's so funny about pancakes?" asked Nathan.

The two laughed even louder.

Chris stopped first and patted Alissa on the knee. "Congratulations. Again."

"For what?"

"For being a hero."

The humor drained from Alissa. "I'm anything but a hero. Everyone on that island is dead."

"Not everyone." Chris motioned to those seated around the table. "They'd all be dead if you didn't insist on going back for them."

"I got a lot of people killed in the process."

"Stop beating yourself up over that. We're in the middle of an apocalypse. People are going to die. Millions of them. You can't prevent that. All you can do is save whoever you can. Fifteen people are alive right now who otherwise would be dead if it not for you."

Alissa looked over at Susie. "I suppose."

"What about Kiera and Little Stevie, and their parents. And Connie?"

Her eyes opened wide. "Jesus, I forgot about them. Miriam must be frantic with worry."

"She'll get over worry a lot quicker than grief. Even more important, we went back to Boston and retrieved those blood samples, so now the government can create the vaccine against the virus. Do you still think you're *not* a hero?"

"I guess," mumbled Alissa, knowing Chris had a point, although she still did not view herself as a hero.

"Wait a minute." Nathan sat up, groaning as he did so. "We went back to Boston?"

"We did." Chris pointed between himself and Alissa. "You stayed on the island with Kiera and Rebecca."

"How long was I out?"

Alissa shrugged. "Two or three days?"

"What happened while I was unconscious?"

"Do you remember the deader attack on the cabin?" asked Chris.

"Yes." Nathan's eyes widened. "And being bitten. Why haven't I turned."

"You fought off the virus, but you're not immune to it."

"That's why we had to go back to Mass General and retrieve the blood samples," added Alissa. "It's the key to the vaccine."

"What vaccine? And how did we get to Maine?"

"We drove."

Chris nudged Alissa. "He slept through the stampede. Remember?"

"Stampede?"

"We were nearly killed by a herd of stampeding deaders."

"How did you get shot?"

Chris glanced down at his wound. "A Marine shot me."

"Actually," corrected Alissa, "you were wounded by a ricochet."

"My version sounds more dramatic."

The nonchalant way they discussed the events drove Nathan nuts. "When were you planning on telling me all this?"

"We've been kind of busy." Alissa had a tone of humorous sarcasm to her voice.

"Don't worry. You can go on the next venture alone." Chris patted his wounded leg. "I'll have to sit that one out."

Alissa smiled, took one of their hands in hers, and squeezed lovingly.

Costas came down from the pilothouse. "Miss Madison, can you join us on the bridge?"

"Anything wrong?"

"No, ma'am. Just a strategy discussion."

When she arrived in the pilothouse, Hoskins stood by the plotting table examining a map. He waved her over.

"You wanted to see me?"

"Yes. We have a slight problem."

"What?"

"According to this chart of the area, the closest dock to Belfast Airport is over two miles away. Even if we landed as close to the airport as possible, it's over a mile to get there. That's going to be tough enough in two and a half feet of snow with Susie and Chris. At least he's mobile. Nathan and Saunders aren't going to be able to walk that far on their own. And that's not even factoring in deaders."

"Did you see any when you were at the airport?" asked Costas.

"No. But then the blizzard was at its height."

"We still have the problem of Susie and the wounded," said Hoskins.

"It's a shame we can't drive there." Costas sighed. "It's only a few miles."

Alissa smiled. "I think I can arrange that. Patricia, take us to Lincolnville."

THIRTY MINUTES LATER, Patricia brought the tug alongside the dock at Lincolnville and idled the engine. Woody and Ben jumped off and secured the mooring lines to the dock as Hoskins' troops provided cover.

Alissa, Hoskins, and Woody examined the area inside the perimeter walls with a pair of binoculars they found in the pilothouse. On the way in, they spotted a dozen deaders sauntering around the southern façade of the barricade and assumed twice as many were nearby unable to be seen, probably attracted by the fighting that had taken place on the island. None were inside the perimeter that they could see. However, after the incident at the marina, they assumed more may be buried under the snow.

"Shit," mumbled Hoskins.

"What's wrong, sir?"

"There are only two Humvees left and the gate is down. The men there must have abandoned their posts when they assumed the island had fallen."

"We still have the two Humvees," said Alissa.

"There's not enough room in them for everyone. Half of us will have to walk."

"It's at least five miles to Belfast," added Woody.

"We don't have any other options."

The M1150 Assault Breacher Vehicle stood in the center of the parking lot.

"Do any of you know how to drive that thing?" asked Alissa.

Hoskins shook his head. "I wish. My men are all ground pounders."

"I might be able to," said Woody.

"Were you in armor?"

"No. But I'm certified to drive forklifts and bulldozers. The concept is the same."

Hoskins thought for a minute. "Do you think you're up to it?"

Woody grinned. "It beats walking."

"I'm sold," said Alissa. "Let's do this."

Five minutes later, they had formulated a plan and briefed everyone. As the others prepared, those with weapons checked their ammo supply and redistributed it evenly. They were down to one spare magazine plus what they still had in their carbines. There were only two spare magazines for the Sig Sauers which Alissa carried since her weapon had a suppressor.

As the others waited on deck, Hoskins' team climbed onto the dock to retrieve the vehicles. Woody and Ben led the way, the former carrying an ice breaker they found aboard ship and the latter a hook on the end of a long pole, both men prodding the snow ahead of them for any deaders concealed under it. Murphy and Ames stayed close for support while Shithead walked between them, sniffing for danger. Alissa, Hoskins, and Costas brought up the rear.

It took ten minutes to reach the M1150. Hoskins climbed up on the vehicle, opened the turret hatch, and peered inside. He banged on the armor. No response.

"It's clear," he whispered.

Woody climbed into the driver's seat while Ben stood in the open turret hatch.

Hoskins crawled down to the chassis to talk with Woody. "Wait until we start the Humvees before firing it up."

"Gotcha."

The others made their way across the parking lot to the Humvees, this time with Murphy and Ames prodding the snow ahead of them. When they reached the two vehicles, Costas provided cover as Alissa opened the doors, checking inside for deaders. The Humvees were empty. Alissa climbed behind the driver's seat of the first vehicle and Costas the second. Both engines started on the first try.

A chorus of moans echoed from the other side of the barricade. The living dead would be upon them in minutes.

Alissa checked her fuel gauge. "I have over half a tank."

"More than enough to get to Belfast." Hoskins stepped back and called to Costas. "What's your fuel situation?"

"Three quarters of a tank."

"Perfect. You two have this?"

Alissa and Costas responded in the affirmative.

"Then let's do it."

Alissa and Costas performed a U-turn in the parking lot and drove down the dock to the tug.

Hoskins and Ames rushed back to the M1150. Woody had started it. Both soldiers climbed on board, the lieutenant replacing Ben in the commander's hatch. By now, the first three deaders had crossed the drawbridge into the compound. Hoskins placed the helmet to the tank's Combat Vehicle Crewman integrated communications system over his ears and spoke into the microphone.

"Woody, can you hear me?"

"Loud and clear."

"Back up the end of the dock. I'll guide you."

Woody slowly maneuvered the tank in reverse. At first, the vehicle went in the wrong direction and jerked, slamming Hoskins' waist into the cupola of the hatch. After a few minutes, he got the hang of operating it and reversed more smoothly. With the lieutenant guiding him, Woody centered himself along the centerline of the dock. At the last second, he veered right and cut left, stopping the M1150 at the beginning of the dock so nothing could get past.

"That's good."

Ames, who stood behind him on the turret, tapped the lieutenant's shoulder. Hoskins lowered the headphones.

"What do we do now, sir?"

Hoskins watched the pack of deaders, now numbering fourteen, stagger toward them. "We sit tight and wait."

ALISSA STOPPED HER Humvee by the tug and jumped out,

leaving the engine running. Costas did the same. Boyce and
Patricia helped Saunders over the gunwale onto the dock, at
which point the medic supported the commanding officer as he
limped to the second Humvee. He placed Saunders in one of
the rear seats then took the adjacent one. Patricia rode
shotgun, the Glock clutched between her hands. Robson curled
up on the back deck along with Susie.

Alissa and Rebecca assisted Nathan to the first Humvee
while Kiera helped Chris, a huge grin on her face.

"I can walk on my own," protested Chris.

"Don't be so macho."

"I thought you liked me being macho."

Kiera blushed with embarrassment. She helped Chris into
one of the rear seats then took her usual position in front.

"Damn it," she muttered, closing the door behind them.

"What's wrong?"

"There's no machine gun."

Chris chuckled. "You're having way too much fun."

Alissa opened the rear hatch and helped Nathan inside.

"Another Humvee?" he protested good-naturedly.

"Sorry. All the limos were booked."

"An ambulance would be nice."

"You can lodge a complaint with Miracle Air."

"Who?"

"I'll explain later. Where's Shithead?"

Glancing around, she saw the dog ten feet away hunched
down by one of the moorings, doing his business. When
finished, he sniffed the pile, lifted his left rear leg, and pissed.
Alissa whistled. Shithead broke into a run, bounding through
the snow, his tail wagging, as if on a country walk. He jumped
into the back deck and shook himself off, splattering Nathan in
melted snow.

"Thanks," said Nathan.

Shithead apologized by giving him a face bath.

Alissa closed the hatch and climbed back into the driver's

seat. Rebecca joined Chris in back.

The two drivers performed three-point turns and headed back to the parking area.

BY NOW, THE fourteen deaders had surrounded the M1150, clutching at Hoskins and Ames, but posing no immediate threat. Twelve more sauntered across the parking lot.

Costas tapped the lieutenant and pointed to the Humvees approaching, "They're here, sir."

Hoskins placed the headphones back over his ears.

"Woody, do you know how to get to Belfast Airport?"

"Sure do."

"Then let's roll."

The M1150 lurched forward and headed across the parking lot, crushing seven deaders beneath its treads. Woody cautiously made his way to the drawbridge, running over four more of the living dead. The two Humvees followed. The surviving deaders staggered after the convoy.

Once across the drawbridge and on open road, Woody became more confident and accelerated, increasing speed to thirty miles per hour. He turned north on Route One. They drove for twelve miles, passing snow-covered fields that seemed like postcards. And not a deader in sight.

Thirty minutes later, they entered Belfast. By now, the storm had stopped, with only a few flurries drifting to the ground. Off to the east, the dark clouds had started to break, revealing a few patches of blue sky. Night would fall in about two hours.

At the airport, Woody turned left and brought the convoy to the terminal building. As they parked, Carrington, Sparks, and the civilians came out to greet them.

Sparks ran up to Robson. "We thought you were dead after we lost contact with you."

"We ran into unexpected problems."

"Did you rescue the survivors?"

Carrington interrupted. "Let's get everybody inside and settled. They can brief us later."

AMENITIES AT THE terminal were scarce. No blankets. Only a few comfortable seats to sit on. And no food, those who had arrived two days ago having eaten what few items remained in the vending machine. They found coffee in the break room but, with no electricity to run the water pumps or coffee maker, they were out of luck. The only water available came from melted snow.

Still, it was preferable to being stuck on Warren Island surrounded by deaders.

The civilians not rescued that day had asked that Nathan be isolated in the break room, most of them fearing he would turn into one of the living dead and attack them. Carrington knew better but asked Nathan if he would agree, explaining he already had enough problems keeping them calm after what had happened. Nathan had no problem with it.

While everyone else briefed the doctor on what had gone down during the rescue mission, Alissa stayed with Nathan and filled him in on the past three days. Beginning with his being infected but not reanimated by the virus. Then she went into detail about the trip to Warren Island, the encounter with the stampeding deaders and their rescue by the National Guard, the mission to Boston to retrieve the vaccine, and the escape from Warren Island, leaving out the sexual tryst with Chris at Mass General. Nathan said nothing during her explanation. When she finished, he stared at her disapprovingly.

"What is it?" asked Alissa.

"You risked four lives to save me after I had been bitten?"

"Yes."

"What were you thinking?"

"That I didn't want to lose you," Alissa protested.

"Not only did you put Chris, Kiera, and Rebecca in danger, you left Miriam and Steve all alone with Little Stevie and Connie?"

"Yes." This time her protestation had less emphasis.

"Why didn't you shoot me?"

"We would have if you turned, but you didn't. That's when I decided to get you medical help. Dr. Carrington thought they might be able to use your blood to develop a vaccine for the deader virus."

"But you didn't know that when you left the cabin, did you?"

Alissa averted her gaze.

"Let me guess," continued Nathan. "You planned on driving me to the island by yourself but Chris and Kiera wouldn't let you go alone."

"Yes."

Nathan leaned his head back against the wall and sighed, an expression that quickly transformed into a chuckle.

"What's so funny?" asked Alissa.

"You could stick your hand into a bucket of shit and pull out a Rolex, that's how lucky you are."

"So, you're not mad at me?"

"A little, but it doesn't matter. Does the doc really think he can develop a vaccine from that blood you got from Boston?"

"He's certain of it."

"Then it all worked out for the best and you came out on top."

"Thanks." Alissa took Nathan's hands in her own. "Let me ask you a question. If the roles were reversed and I had been bitten but not turned, would you have done the same thing for me?"

"Rationally, no. I would never endanger four people to save one probably dead already. Emotionally, though, there's a good chance I would have taken the risk, especially since it was you."

Alissa smiled, not only because of what Nathan had said, but because the disagreement had ended in a draw.

Nathan let go of her hand. "Did Chris try to blow up anything at the hospital or on the island?"

"No, I didn't," answered Chris as he entered the break room along with Hoskins, Robson, Woody, and Sparks.

"Really?" Alissa teased. "What about the grenades at the hospital?"

Nathan's eyes widened. "You used grenades inside a hospital?"

"Yes, but there were extenuating circumstances." Chris raised his hand to end the teasing. "We came to talk to you because we have another problem."

Robson stepped forward. "Now that the storm has let up, the chances are good the *Iwo Jima* will send a search party to look for us in the morning."

"What's the problem with that?" she asked.

"We can't communicate with them," answered Sparks. "The terminal's radio is useless because we have no power, and the radios on the Humvees don't have the range. Our only way to communicate with a rescue party would be through visual contact."

"What about lighting some fires?" suggested Alissa. "There have to be some fifty-five-gallon drums around here we can use."

"That won't work," said Woody. "The center of Warren Island is over twenty miles away. It's doubtful a rescue helicopter would even notice such a small fire."

"Even if they did," added Robson, "it's doubtful the pilot would even pay attention to it being so small."

Hoskins nodded. "Once they see the destruction on the island and the wreck of the Seahawk, they'll assume we're dead and leave."

"Assuming the rescue mission leaves without finding us,

what options do we have?" asked Nathan.

"Damn few," answered Hoskins. "There are no other military installations left in New England. The closest I'm aware of is in up-state New York, and we haven't heard from them in a while. We could drive around, hopefully find a place with a working radio to contact the *Iwo Jima*, but with all this snow and not knowing what the deader situation is like out there, doing that would be like shooting craps at Vegas. And Saunders won't last that long. Without proper medical care, Boyce says he'll be dead in a week to ten days."

"Shit." So much for Alissa's good luck.

"There's an old traffic control tower a few hundred feet from here," said Sparks. "We're going up to see if we can find any solutions. Would you join us?"

"Sure."

THE AIR TRAFFIC control tower Sparks had mentioned was a relic from the 1960s. It stood two hundred feet in height, all metal, with an exposed exterior staircase leading to the control booth, a room with windows covering all four sides. The tower had been abandoned in the late 1980s when the number of flights into Belfast decreased. Now it stood as a rusty hulk, the insides long since gutted and the glass windows broken. It only existed because of a dispute among the town council between those who viewed it as an eyesore and wanted to rip it down and those who wanted to preserve it as part of the town's history, a debate that died along with billions of people during the apocalypse.

Alissa, Hoskins, Sparks, Robson, and Woody climbed the ladder to the control room. The higher they went the more the wind cut through them. They finally reached the top landing and stepped inside, decreasing the gusts only slightly. A flock of birds nesting in the corner, startled by the intrusion, flew out the empty panes, leaving behind a flurry of feathers. Despite being open to the air, the control room stank of bird shit, which covered the floor half an inch in depth. The group ignored the mess and crossed over to the side of the tower looking out over Belfast.

The town ran north along the western banks of Belfast Bay, starting out east of the airport as a small residential area and gradually becoming more populated farther to the north. Even in the dimming light of dusk, deaders could be seen meandering through the streets, oblivious to the food thousands of feet away. Luckily, none of the living dead lurked around the airport.

"Do you see anything we can set on fire?" asked Robson.

"Yeah," answered Sparks. "There's several buildings we could set fire to."

Hoskins shook his head. "Too risky. In this wind, the flames could take out the whole town."

"I've lived through one firestorm," said Alissa. "That's more than enough for me."

"What about lighting off the gas station?" suggested Sparks.

"Same problem," said Woody. "The explosion would be seen for miles but runs the risk of spreading."

As the others explored their options, Alissa made her way to the portion of the tower looking to the south. Her interest piqued.

"What's over there?"

The others joined her.

"That's the Belfast Transfer Station," said Woody.

"In English," asked Robson.

"It's the town dump and recycling center."

"I'm correct in assuming that the mound is a pile of old tires?"

"Yeah." The realization suddenly struck Woody. "I see what you're getting at."

Alissa smiled. "Gentlemen, we found our bonfire."

Chapter Fourteen

C APTAIN EVANS STOOD on the bridge of the *Iwo Jima* as it sailed north toward Warren Island. The storm had dissipated over the past few hours, a small plus. It worried him that they had not heard from anyone on Warren Island or the missing Seahawk in over twenty-four hours. He feared no one had survived.

Lieutenant Commander Channing joined him on the bridge.

"Any word from our missing people?"

"Nothing yet, sir. Comm has been trying to reach them for hours. We're monitoring all frequencies for traffic, military as well as civilian."

"Damn it." Evans waved Channing closer. "We've been ordered by the acting president to deploy to the Gulf of Mexico and resume rescue operations there. With Warren Island gone, we no longer have any units in the northeast."

"What about any survivors in the area?"

"The president doesn't feel it's worth the expense of resources. Our groups west of the Mississippi can help anyone who requests it."

"What should we do about our missing people?"

The captain thought for a moment. "Send a helicopter to the island in the morning. If anyone is alive, we'll extract them. If not, then any survivors are on their own."

"Yes, sir. Let's hope for the best."

And expect the worst, thought Evans.

ALISSA SLEPT RESTLESSLY that night, which did not surprise her, even though they were in a relatively safe location. She recalled dreaming although she could not remember the details, assuming they must have been of the days before the apocalypse since they left her with a sense of happiness. When Hoskins shook her awake an hour before dawn, she experienced that momentary disappointment when the desires of her dreams gave way to the nightmare of reality.

"Miss Madison, we're heading out. Did you still want to join us?"

"Of course." Alissa met his gaze then blinked a few times.

"Are you okay?"

"I'm fine," lied Alissa. The vision in her left eye was blurred. Not blurred. A dark spot in the center of her eye blocked approximately one-tenth of her vision. She focused on the embroidered nametag on Hoskins' chest and closed her left eye. She read the name with no problem. When she closed her right eye, the nametag and the area around it were blacked out.

"Are you sure?"

"I just woke up, that's all."

"The others are waiting for us."

Alissa had been laying by Nathan, who had fallen asleep. She kissed him gently on the forehead and followed Hoskins out into the terminal. Woody and Ben had found three plastic five-gallon Jerry cans and filled them with fuel syphoned from the M1150, which now stood by the exit. Woody, Costas, and Ames hovered by the door.

Hoskins addressed the group. "We're heading over to the transfer station to set those tires on fire. Hopefully, it'll attract any rescue missions sent to the island. The rest of you stay here. Corporal, I'm leaving a radio with you. Signal me if there are problems."

Murphy nodded.

"Won't the flames attract deaders?" one of the civilians asked nervously.

"It might, but there doesn't seem to be too many of them in town. Even if there are, they'll be attracted to the flames so you'll be safe as long as you stay quiet." Hoskins turned to his team. "Are we ready?"

"Let's do this," responded Costas.

The corporal led the way out, followed by the others who each carried one of the plastic Jerry cans. Ames brought up the rear.

The stack of tires sat less than half a mile from the terminal. Now that the storm had stopped and the winds died down, the walk had not been as grueling as on Warren Island. It did take longer than usual due to the accumulated snow and being careful about deaders buried under the drifts. They made it to the pile with no incident. Orange streaks tinged the eastern horizon as the sun prepared to dawn. As Costas and Ames took up position on their flanks, the others stepped over to the tires.

Woody pulled three tires off the pile, brushing off the snow and flipping them over to expose the dry side. He stacked them against the others then removed three more tires, placing them so one end sat against the top of the stack and the other on the remaining tires. Taking a Jerry can, he unscrewed the cap and emptied the fuel, saturating the stack and the three tires placed at top. The second can he used to douse the tires surrounding the stack. With the third, he splashed the fuel up the length and side of the pile, creating riverlets of fuel that extended for a hundred feet on both sides and toward the peak. Woody withdrew a lighter from his pocket and turned to the others.

"I'd step back if I were you."

The rest of the team retreated fifty feet.

Woody flicked on the lighter and extended his arm, inching forward until the flame touched the tires. The fuel ignited. The stack instantly burst into flames, spreading to the adjacent tires and working its way along the streaks of fuel. The smell of burning rubber filled their nostrils. Black smoke billowed into the sky.

Woody picked up two of the empty Jerry cans. "Let's head back before the fire attracts deaders."

"Don't we have to keep it going?" asked Alissa.

"That'll burn on its own for days. Let's hope someone from the military sees it."

CAPTAIN JIM ALWELL flew the Super Stallion on a course that took him directly from the *Iwo Jima*, currently circling ten miles off the coast of Maine opposite Penobscot Bay, to Warren Island. He flew at an altitude of five hundred feet. The sky was cloudless, allowing the sun to reflect off the ice flows extending from the various islands in the bay. From up here, the coast looked so beautiful, so pristine, so untouched. It reminded Alwell of a nature documentary. God only knew what they'd find when they reached Islesboro.

The helicopter made landfall at the southern tip of the main island and headed north, following the primary road. Alwell looked for a sign that anyone had survived the outbreak, so far without—

"What happened here?" muttered Lieutenant Anthony Canderossi.

Alwell focused on what the co-pilot had seen. Up ahead looked like a battle zone. It appeared as if a tree had blocked the road and been sawed into bits to make passage. Several sets of tire tracks disturbed the snow. What stood out most were the bodies extending north along the road and the snow drenched crimson in blood. Alwell hovered over the scene as he and Canderossi examined it.

"Are they the living or the dead?" asked the co-pilot.

"Probably a mixture of both. I'm assuming someone survived that skirmish because whatever vehicles made all those tracks are no longer here."

"Which means there may still be survivors."

"Let's hope so."

"Looks like another battle zone over there." Ensign Richard Kerwin, the crew chief, leaned between the two seats and pointed to their eleven o'clock position.

The pilot flew forward and hovered over the edge of the tree line. A neon red cross, much of the glass shattered, sat above the main entrance. As with the previous location, tire tracks disturbed the snow and bodies lay in the blood-drenched snow. Something had exploded. The hulk of a burned vehicle sat at the edge of the parking lot. The other vehicles, as well as the front façade of the building, had been ripped apart by shrapnel. Again, none of the vehicles that had made the tracks were present. Several deaders sauntered through the area, glancing up at the Super Stallion and reaching for it.

Alwell removed from the console the microphone to the exterior loudspeaker. "This is Captain Alwell from the *U.S.S. Iwo Jima*. If there is anyone alive inside the hospital, please let us know and we'll rescue you."

They waited thirty seconds and, when no one responded, the pilot repeated his message. Each of the three men watched the windows and doors, hoping for some indication of life. Nothing.

"We have to assume they're dead or escaped," said Canderossi.

"But to where?" asked Kerwin.

"There are tracks running north and south. Let's see where they lead."

Alwell turned the Super Stallion south and followed the main road. He detoured to the school where the corpses indicated another battle had occurred and issued the same call for survivors, again with no results. Flying back to the main road, he continued until they arrived at the marina. Again, the same battle scene, the same call to survivors, and the same negative response.

This time Alwell headed north. The tracks took them to the airfield.

"There's Robson's Seahawk." Canderossi pointed to the wreck.

Alwell hovered over the wreck and keyed the exterior loud-speaker. "Robson, are you there? This is Captain Alwell."

No response.

Alwell lowered the Super Stallion fifty feet from the crash site and used the downdraft from the rotors to remove the gathered snow over the windscreen of the crashed Seahawk, enabling the crew to view the interior.

"Do you see anything?" asked Alwell.

"Frank's inside the cockpit still strapped to his seat," answered Kerwin. "From the way his neck is dangling, it looks like he snapped it on impact."

"Any sign of Robson?"

"None."

"Shit."

"I saw some more tracks heading west," said Canderossi.

"Let's check it out."

Alwell followed them to the ferry terminal, finding the same indications of battle but no survivors.

"What now?" asked the co-pilot.

"We'll head back to the *Iwo Jima*. Whatever happened down there, no one survived."

"They put up one hell of a fight, though." Kerwin made the sign of the cross.

"We'll do another flyover of the island on our way back, just in case."

Alwell turned to starboard and headed back to the airfield.

Kerwin took a last look out the port window, then did a double take. "Hold on, sir. I spotted something."

"Survivors?"

"I'm not sure. Look to the north."

Alwell brought the Super Stallion around. Approximately fifteen miles north of them, a thick, black pillar of smoke billowed into the sky.

"Do you think it's a signal?" asked Kerwin.

"Something could have caught fire," suggested Canderossi.

"In either case, we're going to check it out."

ALISSA, HOSKINS, AND Woody stood inside the abandoned air traffic control tower. The lieutenant concentrated to the south while Woody made certain no deaders wandered too close to the terminal building. As anticipated, the flames and noise generated by the tire blaze attracted the living dead, though not nearly as many as expected. Most had come from the center of town, crossing the airfield. A few had staggered to within a few hundred feet of the others in the terminal, oblivious to their presence. Alissa watched them mindlessly saunter toward the fire, ending their trek by entering the flames. Their bodies ignited, consumed by the inferno without them even realizing it. For the first time since the outbreak began, she felt pity for the living dead.

She looked away from the nightmare. "What time is it?"

Woody checked his watch. "Almost nine."

"Shouldn't the helicopter have reached the island by now?" she asked.

"*If* it was dispatched." Hoskins rubbed his tired eyes. "Remember, this is a long shot. They may not even expend the resources to search for us."

"I know." The few options left to them if this failed raced through her mind, their number limited and none of them having much chance of success.

"Give it time. If the *Iwo Jima* sent out a rescue mission, it'll spend a lot of time checking the—"

Woody shushed the lieutenant and moved over to the southern side of the tower. "Do you hear that?"

Hoskins shifted his head to the side and listened. "I don't hear anything."

Alissa shook her head. "Neither do…. Wait a minute. I do now. It sounds like—"

"A helicopter." Hoskins scanned the area around the terminal building and, once certain no deaders were nearby, removed the radio from his pocket and keyed the talk button. "Boyce, are you there?"

"Yes, sir."

"Get everyone outside. We have an inbound chopper. Make sure it sees us."

"Roger that."

Hoskins slid the radio into his pocket and headed for the stairs, waving for Alissa and Woody to follow.

AS ALWELL FLEW closer to Belfast, it became apparent that a tire fire on the outskirts of town generated the black smoke.

"There's no way an accident caused that," stated Canderossi.

"Keep your eyes open for survivors."

Alwell slowly maneuvered the Super Stallion toward town, keeping the conflagration to port, as he and the others searched for signs of life. It took only a minute for Kerwin to tap the pilot on the shoulder and point straight ahead.

"Sir, by the airport terminal."

A group of people exited the building onto the tarmac, jumping and waving their arms, hoping to be seen. Alwell flashed the exterior lights to let the survivors know they had been spotted and maneuvered the helicopter in their direction.

"DO THEY SEE US?" asked Susie, her voice tinged with excitement.

"I think so, honey." Patricia hugged the girl, tears of joy running down her cheeks.

Alissa and the others arrived as the Super Stallion hovered overhead. Hoskins ordered everybody back against the wall of the terminal. The helicopter landed one hundred feet from the building, kicking up a whirlwind of snow that lashed at those on the ground. No one cared. It meant they were saved.

The starboard door slid open and the crew chief jumped out, kept his head lowered, and ran over to the group.

"Who's in charge."

"That'd be me. Lieutenant Hoskins. Maine National Guard." He held out his hand.

Kerwin shook it. "How many in your group, sir?"

"Twenty-three."

Shithead barked.

Hoskins smiled and corrected himself. "Twenty-four. Three need medical attention."

"We'll contact *Iwo Jima* and have a medical team waiting for you. I suggest you get on board ASAP before we attract deaders."

"Way ahead of you on that. My people are bringing out the wounded."

Ames and Costas deployed to the front and rear of the Super Stallion while Murphy kept guard at the terminal. Kerwin ushered the others onto the helicopter and got them settled.

"Kiera," said Alissa. "Take Shithead and get on board. I'll wait for Chris and Nathan."

Kiera nodded and joined the others. She looked over her shoulder. "Come on, boy."

Shithead followed, romping through the snow, his tail wagging.

A moment later, the rest of the group emerged from the building. Boyce carried Saunders over his shoulder. Woody and Ben helped Nathan. Chris limped. Alissa followed, sitting between Nathan and Chris.

With everyone on board, Hoskins recalled the rest of his men, being the last to board. Kerwin slid the door shut and made sure everyone was seated, strapped in, and wearing their communications headsets before informing Alwell.

The helicopter lifted off. At an altitude of one thousand feet, Alwell turned south and headed for home.

"Ladies and gentlemen, sit tight. We'll be back on board the *Iwo Jima* in about thirty minutes."

Robson leaned forward and waved to get Alissa's attention. "God damn, you pulled it off."

"What do you mean?"

"Not only did you retrieve the blood samples to make the vaccine, but you saved everyone aboard this helicopter. You're a hero."

"Thanks." Alissa forced a smile. She didn't feel like a hero. All she could think of on the flight back were the dead she left behind in Boston and on Warren Island.

HALF AN HOUR later, the Super Stallion settled down on the deck of the *Iwo Jima*. Most of the civilians applauded. Kerwin helped them remove their headsets and unbuckle themselves, then slid open the starboard door. The ship's medic jumped in.

"Where are the wounded?"

"Right here," said Boyce, pointing to the three men.

"Has anyone been bit?"

"Just this one man, but he's not infected."

"You mean that's Patient Zero?"

Nathan glanced over at Alissa.

"Get used to it," she said. "It's better than being a deader."

Nathan grunted a grudging approval.

Chris gently punched him in the shoulder. "You're famous."

"More like infamous."

The ship's medic and Kerwin assisted the three wounded men off the Super Stallion and onto stretchers where the medical team brought them below.

One by one, the others filed out. As Susie passed, she ran over and hugged Alissa. "Thank you for saving us."

"You're welcome, hon."

The girl broke the embrace, waved at Alissa, and exited the helicopter with Patricia.

Alissa and Kiera were the last non-crew members on board. Alissa wrapped an arm around her shoulder. "Let's go."

Ensign Paul Simon waited for them on deck. "It's good to see you again."

"It's good to be back."

"Come with me, please. We have some hot food and strong coffee waiting for you."

"Before we do that, can we borrow your radio?"

Chapter Fifteen

MIRIAM HAD SPENT the last three days getting the cabin cleaned up, working ten or more hours a day. By the third day, everything had been returned to normal except for the bullet holes in the wall, the broken furniture, the shattered glass and unhinged doors, and the nightmarish memories.

Three feet of snow covered the compound because of yesterday's blizzard, which gave Miriam something else to do as she shoveled off the back deck, the front porch, and a path to the Ram. Little Stevie and Connie joined her and made snowmen, although it disturbed her that the children built deader snowmen attacking human snowmen. Maybe the children were adapting to this brave new world better than the adults. Steve joined her, helping clear off the Ram and shoveling around the tires. Neither of them would attempt to clear the driveway. At least the accumulated snow buried the piles of deader corpses and the remains of the funeral pyre.

Even Archer had attempted to join them but, once on the front porch staring at the mountain of white in front of him, turned around and went back to lay down in front of the fireplace.

After shoveling, Miriam took a hot shower and made lunch. The family voted for tuna fish. Little Stevie and Connie played checkers at the dining room table. Steve sat next to them and read, the radio on the table, waiting for the call from Alissa that seemed less likely to come.

As Miriam opened the cans, Archer raced into the kitchen,

jumped on the counter, and inched his way toward the bowl. Rather than mooch food, he stared at Miriam and meowed pathetically.

"I know. I miss them, too."

Archer meowed again.

"Yes, we're all worried about them." She leaned closer to Archer and he rubbed his head against hers.

"You keep hoping they return, and I'll keep praying, and maybe together we—"

A voice from the radio interrupted her.

"This is Home Plate. I'm trying to reach Alissa's friends in New Hampshire. Do you read me? Over."

Miriam raced out of the kitchen so fast she scared Archer, who ran for cover.

Steve had picked up the microphone. "This is Steve. I read you loud and clear. Over."

"I have someone here who wants to talk to you. Over."

A moment passed before Alissa's voice came through the speakers. "Steve, is that you?"

"Yes. Is everyone all right?"

"They are."

Miriam grabbed the microphone. "Where's Kiera?"

"Right here, mom. I love you."

"I love you, too." Miriam broke down. Steve reached out and rubbed her back. "Are you okay? Were you hurt?"

"I'm fine. I got to fire a machine gun."

"Somehow that doesn't make me feel better." Miriam laughed through her tears. "Why did it take so long for you to call us? We've been worried sick."

Alissa answered. "We've been… busy."

Little Stevie grabbed the microphone. "Hi, Kiera."

"Hi, Stevie. I have the toy Spiderman you gave me. It was the perfect good luck charm. I'll give it back when I see you."

"I gave it to you, so you keep it."

Miriam took back the microphone and hugged Little Stevie

against her. "When will you be back?"

"I don't know yet." Alissa sounded exhausted. "We just made it to the *Iwo Jima* and plans haven't been decided yet. It should be soon."

"How did you wind up on a Navy vessel?"

"It's a long story. I'll fill you in later."

"How's Nathan?"

"He's conscious and feeling better, but still rundown from his infection. Chris was wounded in the leg. Rebecca and Kiera are fine, and so is Shithead."

Archer jumped up onto the table and meowed loudly.

"Archer, it's mommy. I'll be home soon."

The cat stepped over to the radio and rubbed his head against the speaker.

"Miriam, are you still there?"

"I'm here."

"We need to get settled in and rest. It's been a long three days. I'll contact you tomorrow and let you know what the plans are."

"Sounds good. And Kiera?"

"Yeah?"

"Be careful, please."

"Yes, mom." Even over the radio, she expressed the typical teenage frustration with a concerned parent.

"Talk to you soon," said Alissa. "Over and out."

Miriam placed the microphone on the table and sobbed. Little Stevie and Connie hugged her tightly. "Everything is okay, Aunt Miriam."

Miriam hugged them back. Kiera and the others were alive and safe, and that was all that mattered.

ALISSA PLACED DOWN the microphone and turned to the ship's radio operator. "Thank you for letting me contact my friends."

"No problem, ma'am. The captain said you can use it any time you want."

She turned to Sparks. "And thank you for helping us."

"It's the least I can do. None of us would be alive if not for you. Come on, I'll show you where the mess hall is."

"I'm starving," said Kiera.

"So am I," added Rebecca.

"I'll pass. I want to sleep."

"Suit yourself, ma'am." Sparks led them into the corridor.

Outside the radio room, Rebecca paused and took Alissa's hands. "I know you don't enjoy all the attention, but don't sell yourself short. A lot of people are alive today and, once the vaccine is developed, a lot of people will survive this outbreak who might not have otherwise, because of you."

She kissed Rebecca on the cheek. "Thank you."

Alissa led Shithead back to their quarters. As much as she hated to admit it, the others were right. Sure, she had made some dangerous decisions, some of them bad, but things were no longer the way they had been six months ago. However, she had adapted to this post-apocalypse world and had wound up doing well despite everything. She had good friends who believed in her and followed her, and together they had made a considerable difference. The others were right. She needed to cast aside her self-doubt and realize she would not be able to save everyone, that sudden and violent death had become the new norm. She had seen the group through quite a lot so far and would continue to do so until this nightmare ended.

Once back in their quarters, Alissa crawled into her bunk. Shithead joined her, pushing until she lay against the bulkhead, and then settled down, snuggling against her. Alissa wrapped an arm around the dog. His tail wagged, banging against her leg. She did not mind. It reminded her that she was alive and should enjoy the little pleasures in life while she could.

Alissa and Shithead dozed off. Alissa slept for the next six-teen hours, a deep and restful slumber in which she dreamt of life before the outbreak and wondered what the future had in store.

It was the first good sleep she had gotten in over three days.

PREVIEW OF
NURSE ALISSA VS. THE ZOMBIES VII:
ON THE ROAD

A LISSA WOKE UP slowly. She lay there, her eyes closed, as she transitioned out of sleep. She remembered dozing off in a safe location. After a few minutes, the constant hum and the steady, low vibrations reminded her she was aboard the Amphibious Assault Ship *U.S.S. Iwo Jima* off the coast of New England.

Alissa recalled falling asleep with a large, furry, bed-hogging bunk mate. Shithead no longer pushed her against the cold bulkhead. She reached out and felt around the mattress, but he had moved. Finally opening her eyes, she checked the floor. At some point, Shithead had abandoned her and now lay a few bunks down with Kiera, snuggling close to the teenager and snoring.

No light filtered in through the porthole, which didn't surprise her. Alissa felt like she had slept for hours. The straining in her bladder confirmed it. As she pushed aside the covers, something weighing them down caught her attention. A pair of dark blue coveralls sat folded on the end of the bunk along with a towel, a small bottle of shampoo, and a bar of soap, the latter two resting on top of a note. She pulled it out and read it.

Alissa.

The captain gave each of us a change of clothes. I guess we smell ripe.

Kiera

Alissa glanced down at her clothes. Ripe would be an understatement. She had become so used to be covered in deader blood she barely noticed it anymore. Her current outfit, including her boots and leather coat, were soiled with the remains of the living and the living dead. Even her hands had ground in streaks of red from the blood. Besides, she could use a hot shower to relax her muscles that were tight and achy from two days of combat.

Swinging her legs out of the bunk and picking up the clean clothes and toiletries, Alissa made her way to the showers. Once in the lit corridor, Alissa blinked her left eye several time. Not only had the black spot from yesterday not gone away, but it had also grown larger, now effecting nearly twenty-five percent of her vision. She would check it out later that morning.

Only a few people were in the showers. She stripped down and took a long, semi-warm shower. Not that it mattered. It felt good to be clean again. Judging by the amount of blood and dirt that swirled down the drain, she needed it. When finished, she slid on her old underwear and the new clothes, which were a little loose. The rest she dumped in the trash.

After dropping off the towel and toiletries back at her bunk, Alissa made her way to the mess hall. The breakfast line had started to form. The aroma drifting from the kitchen made her stomach rumble. At 0500, the doors opened and the line moved forward. The cooks served scrambled eggs, bacon, and potatoes. She took a huge helping of each, plus an orange juice and cup of coffee. Entering the mess, she saw Patricia and Susie seated at a table, the former also in dark blue coveralls, the latter still in what she had worn on the island. Alissa made their way over to them.

"Mind if I join you?"

Susie beamed. "Have a seat."

Alissa sat down. "How's the food?"

Susie shrugged. "It's okay, but it's not as good as IHOP."

Patricia leaned over and hugged the girl. "You must be rested."

"Why do you say that?" Alissa scooped some eggs into her mouth.

"You slept sixteen hours."

"That long?"

"You needed it."

"And you snore," added Susie.

Alissa almost spit out her eggs trying not to laugh. "Are you sure it wasn't Shithead?"

"He snores, too. But not as loud as you."

"Susie," Patricia politely chastised the girl. "You don't say things like that. It's not nice."

Susie pouted. "Sorry, Aunt Alissa."

"That's all right." Alissa leaned closer and gave Susie a conspiratorial wink. "I know it's true."

"Aunt Alissa, what's going to happen to us now?"

"I don't know."

"Kiera says you own a cabin in the woods in New Hampshire. Can we stay with you?"

With all that had gone on the past few days, she had not given much thought to what would happen after their rescue from Warren Island. She had no idea how her team would get back to North Conway.

"I think we can arrange that."

"Really?" Susie asked excitedly.

"Yes." Alissa paused. "Could you do me a favor and get me a glass of iced water?"

"Sure." Susie bolted from the table.

When she was out of earshot, Alissa leaned closer to Patricia. "I don't mind taking you both with me, but does Susie have any other family she should go to?"

Patricia shook her head. "Susie's parents had her late in life. Both sets of grandparents are dead. Her father had two brothers. One was killed in a car accident three years ago along

139

with his entire family. The other lives in California with his family, but no one knows what happened to them since the outbreak."

"What about you?"

"My husband, Phil, died trying to save Susie's family. His parents are dead. He has a brother who lives in Arizona and a sister in Philadelphia, but we haven't heard from them. I'm an only child and my parents retired to Orlando. The chances of any of them having survived this are nil. Besides, I'm all Susie has. We stick together."

"Good for you. I promise I'll take care of both of you."

"Thank you." Patricia reached out and held Alissa's hand.

Susie ran up. "I have your iced water."

"Thank you." Alissa took a long drink. The three chatted about anything they could think of except deaders. As Alissa ate, she described to Susie the cabin, Little Stevie and Connie, and Archer.

"You have a cat?"

Alissa nodded. He's a bit of an asshat, but he loves children."

"I can't wait to meet him."

"You will soon."

"Excuse me, ma'am?"

A young seaman stood behind her.

"Yes?"

"Are you Miss Madison?"

"I am."

"Warrant Officer Marlowe, ma'am. The captain would like to see you on the bridge."

"That sounds ominous," teased Patricia.

"Nothing to be worried about. He just wants to discuss with you your options for the future."

"Go ahead," said Patricia. We'll take care of your tray."

"Thanks." Alissa stood. "Lead the way."

A Thank You to My Readers

I've been writing for as long as I can remember. It's one of the most fulfilling things I've done with my life. I love sitting on my front porch or in my back yard, surrounded by nature while writing, often with Walther and Bella sitting beside me or getting into trouble.

The best part is having fans who read my books and enjoy them. I'm extremely fortunate and grateful that I have a fanbase that devours my novels like zombies eating human flesh. You keep reading and I'll keep writing.

If you liked *Nurse Alissa vs. the Zombies VI: Rescue,* or any of the other books in the series, please post a review on Amazon. It doesn't have to be long—just a rating and a sentence or two about why you enjoyed it. The more reviews the series receives, the more opportunity other readers have of discovering the book.

The *Nurse Alissa* saga will continue. The next book in the series is currently in production and the plans are to make Alissa's life miserable well into 2021, maybe even 2022. I have some unique situations planned for Alissa's team and some interesting characters they'll run into.

A new series, which is more along the lines of paranormal horror, is currently in the works. The first book, The Ghosts of Eden Hollow, is scheduled for release in late February. In addition, plans are moving ahead on that non-zombie, post-apocalypse series I was talking about earlier.

So, hang on. This year is going to be exciting.

Acknowledgments

Writing is solitary and lonely. Getting a book published is a complicated process involving many people, all of whom deserve to be recognized.

I want to thank my Beta readers, the unsung heroes of writers. No matter how many times you edit and proofread your manuscript, errors always slip through. My Beta readers, especially Dan Uebel and Doc Fried, provide detailed notes on the spelling, grammatical, or punctuation mistakes I missed and help me not to look illiterate.

Once again, a major debt of thanks goes to James R. Jackson, a former U.S. Navy Chief Petty Officer and author of the *Up From the Depths* series. As with my previous *Nurse Alissa* novel, there is a heavy military element in this book. Being a civilian, I reached out for assistance. James read the manuscript and provided numerous suggestions on how to bring the book in line with military policies and procedures. This book would have read a lot less realistic if not for James. However, certain protocols I had to abandon for the sake of the plot, so any scenes that don't pass the guffaw factor are my responsibility.

Christian Bentulan designed the cover art for *Nurse Alissa vs. the Zombies VI: Rescue* as well as the other books in the saga. I love Christian's work. His covers reach out and grab the reader's attention as well as foreshadow what is to come within the pages.

You would not be reading this book, or any of the others in the *Nurse Alissa* series, were it not for my dear friend and colleague, Alina Giuchici. I hadn't written a zombie series since

Rotter Apocalypse was published in 2015. Alina is a major fan of my stories and kept urging me to go back to writing about the living dead. With some gentle shoving in the right direction and a few well-placed ideas, over the course of a long week on the road I came up with the concept of the Alissa series. If you like these books, be sure to thank Alina.

Finally, a major debt of thanks goes to my family, human and furry. As with my last five novels, I wrote, edited, and released this one during the COVID-19 lockdown, taking advantage of having so much time on my hands and being stuck at home. This has been the best year of the dogs' lives because they think I stay home all day to be with them, and they want to spend every minute with me. The cats are pissed off that I'm around all the time, especially Archer whose naps are disturbed by my typing. (Yes, Alissa's Archer is taken directly from my own cat Archer, especially his asshattery.) It's hard to maintain my writing discipline when everyone is home, and even harder to maintain my sanity when there is nowhere to go, but I couldn't do this without their love and support.

About the Author

Scott M. Baker was born and raised in Everett, Massachusetts and spent twenty-three years in northern Virginia working for the Central Intelligence Agency. Scott is now retired and lives just outside of Concord, New Hampshire with his wife and fellow writer Alison Beightol, stepdaughter, two rambunctious boxers, and two cats who treat him as their human servant. He has written six books in the *Nurse Alissa vs. the Zombies* saga, his latest zombie apocalypse series; the *Shattered World* series, his five-book, young adult post-apocalypse series about a group of adventurers attempting to close portals into Hell; *The Vampire Hunters* trilogy, about humans fighting the undead in Washington D.C.; *Rotter World*, *Rotter Nation*, and *Rotter Apocalypse*, his post-apocalyptic zombie saga; *Yeitso*, his homage to the giant monster movies of the 1950s that he loved watching as a kid; as well as several zombie-themed novellas and anthologies.

Please check out Scott's social media accounts for the latest information on future books, upcoming events, and other fun stuff.

Blog: scottmbakerauthor.blogspot.com
Facebook: facebook.com/groups/397749347486177
MeWe: mewe.com/i/scottmbaker
Twitter: twitter.com/vampire_hunters
Instagram: instagram.com/scottmbakerwriter
TikTok: tiktok.com/@scottbaker666

Made in United States
Troutdale, OR
11/15/2024

24868266R00086